ASA:
THE GIRL WHO
TURNED INTO
A PAIR OF
CHOPSTICKS

Natsuko Imamura was born in Hiroshima, Japan, in 1980. Her fiction has won various prestigious Japanese literary prizes, including the Noma Literary New Face Prize, the Mishima Yukio Prize and the Akutagawa Prize. She lives in Osaka with her husband and daughter.

ASA: THE GIRL WHO TURNED INTO A PAIR OF CHOPSTICKS

NATSUKO IMAMURA

Translated from the Japanese by Lucy North

faber

First published in 2024
by Faber & Faber Ltd
The Bindery, 51 Hatton Garden
London EC1N 8HN

Typeset by Faber & Faber Ltd
Printed in the UK by CPI Group (UK) Ltd, Croydon, CR0 4YY

A CIP record for this book
is available from the British Library

ISBN 978-0-571-38413-6

MIX
Paper | Supporting
responsible forestry
FSC® C171272

Printed and bound in the UK on FSC® certified paper in line with our continuing
commitment to ethical business practices, sustainability and the environment.
For further information see faber.co.uk/environmental-policy

2 4 6 8 10 9 7 5 3

CONTENTS

ASA:
THE GIRL WHO
TURNED INTO
A PAIR OF
CHOPSTICKS

Asa lived with her mother in a small rented apartment. Behind their building was a big field of sunflowers. One day, Asa's mother came home with a plastic carrier bag filled with sunflower seeds: their landlord had given them to her for free. After laying out a sheet of newspaper in the middle of the floor, Asa and her mother worked steadily, over many days, to peel off their husks. Asa's mother then took the hulled seeds and tossed them in a frying pan, sprinkled them with salt – and they turned into something nice for Asa to eat. At the kitchen table, Asa leaned over, picked up some seeds, dropped them in her mouth, and chewed, savouring the flavour. Occasionally, a little lump of salt got in, and she asked her mother at the sink for a glass of water. Then she returned to the pile, and carried on snacking.

'I want to take some of these to daycare!' Asa said, licking the salt off her fingers.

3

Next morning, her mother put a stuffed brown envelope into her hands. 'Don't just keep these to yourself. You've got to share them with your friends.'

Hiding behind the pedal organ in the daycare-centre classroom Asa beckoned her best friend Rumi-chan to come over.

'What have you got?' Rumi-chan asked.

'Look!' Asa held out the stained envelope.

Rumi-chan put her face close. Asa opened up the top, and Rumi-chan peered inside.

'What is it?'

'Sunflower seeds!'

Rumi-chan had never heard of sunflowers having seeds. 'Sunflowers?' She cocked her head.

Asa plucked out a seed and popped it in her own mouth.

'Oh! You ate it!'

'You can eat these.'

'Do they taste good?'

'Yes!'

'You're going to get a tummy ache.'

'You try one.'

Rumi-chan shook her head. 'Nuh-uh.'

'They're so good!' Asa said. Tipping the envelope, she shook it. The seeds flowed smoothly out into her palm. She held out her hand. 'Have one.'

'I don't want to.'

'Why not? They're nice!'

'No.'

'Why? Just try one.'

'I said no!'

'Rumi-chan . . .'

'Naw!' Rumi-chan said. 'Naw! I don't want to!' And she pushed Asa's hands away, and headed out to the playground with a skipping rope.

When Asa entered primary school, they moved to live with Asa's maternal grandmother. Here Asa came across all sorts of things that had never been a part of her old life: a sofa, a rug, a TV remote, a shower, a microwave . . . In her first year, Asa made cookies – it was the first time she had ever done such a thing, so her mother helped. Her grand-mother said she had only used the shiny new oven once. Asa wanted to give home-made cookies as a goodbye present to a popular boy in her class, Yamazaki Shun-kun, who was about to leave and go to another school. At the start of term when chores had been allocated through the rock-paper-scissors game, she and Shun-kun had been charged with looking after lost property. They had confided in each other: if only they had been put on the pet-care team!

The cookies were perfect. Raisins and nuts. What a good idea it had been to combine them. She wanted to devour ten cookies on the spot, but she exercised super-strong willpower and put the cookies in a paper bag, then decorated it with a pink ribbon.

The next day, Asa held out the cookies to Shun-kun. 'Please eat these.' But the gift was immediately pushed back. She had neglected to do her research. Shun-kun didn't like nuts, and he didn't like raisins, in fact he hated cookies, and he found it terrifying even to look at them. Shun-kun ran away from her. 'Stay well!' Asa called, waving after him.

Sometime later, Asa had another try, again with her mother by her side. This time, Asa didn't put nuts in, or raisins, and – since Shun-kun had by now left – she decided to give the cookies to her grandmother. It was Honour the Elderly day. Her grandmother accepted the bag, but she seemed reluctant to eat what it contained. The truth was, her teeth were weak and she was also diabetic. Seeing the little bag left untouched on the table, Asa took it to her mother, but her mother told her sadly that she had to go to the doctor's the next day for a medical examination, and she had been given instructions not to eat.

So Asa had to eat the biscuits all by herself. Her mother had said she would be sure to taste a biscuit when she came home, but she didn't come home and went straight to the hospital, and from then on she was in and out of hospital repeatedly.

In her second year at school, Asa finally got to be put on pet-care duty. This involved feeding the goldfish in a fish tank kept in the classroom.

On the first day, Asa excitedly sprinkled the feed over the water.

'Goldfish! Come and get your food . . .' she called.

But the goldfish just stayed in a huddle in the bottom of the tank.

The next time, Asa again sprinkled the feed but again not a single fish swam up. It couldn't be that they weren't hungry because when Hirai-kun, who was on duty with Asa, sprinkled the flakes, the fish swam to the surface, eagerly gobbling them up. Asa did exactly as Hirai-kun did: she tipped the feed into the palm of one hand, took a pinch with the other, and sprinkled the flakes a few inches above the water. But the fish just didn't want to eat. A class meeting was held. Asa should be taken off the job, people said, or the fish would end up starving to death. Hirai-kun should feed the fish. Asa should just fill in the diary, and clean the tank, skimming the water with a net. While opinions flew, Asa sat silently at a desk by the window at the back of the class, her head lowered, staring at the palms of her hands.

One day, that same year, Asa was on lunch duty. That day's lunch was beef stew, rice, green-bean salad, a little bottle of milk and an apple. Asa had to spoon out the green-bean salad into little bowls. Ten days earlier there had been a poisoning incident at a wedding in a distant town, and more than one hundred people had become very sick – some had even died. The culprit had been green beans, domestically produced ones; nothing to do with the beans the school used, which were grown abroad and delivered from a nearby school lunch centre. Nevertheless, not one person in Asa's class took a bowl of the green-bean salad she had ladled out.

'No way am I going to take any of that!'

'That's scary!'

'We're too young to die yet!'

And her classmates passed straight by. Were they persecuting her? That's certainly what it seemed like.

But that was nothing – not compared to what came later.

The next year, the same sort of thing happened, though now it really was persecution. This time there had been no recent poisoning incident. The menu was vegetable and seafood stir-fry, macaroni salad, rice, a little bottle of milk and a natsu mikan for dessert. Asa dished out bowls of salad, but no one in her cohort at school wanted to touch them – everyone refused. Similar sorts of incidents happened in her fourth year, and in her fifth, and in her sixth.

Her mother went into hospital for another long stay. Determined not to worry her, Asa didn't tell her anything about what was happening at school, nor indeed at home. Now her mother was in hospital, her grandmother had started doing the oddest things – she called Asa 'Setchan', she wet herself outside the toilet, and she picked up the phone when it hadn't rung to talk to somebody who didn't exist. Most painful was when her grandmother accused her of putting poison in her food, and knocked the dishes to the floor. This hurt Asa deeply. She had a visit from her teacher, who had become concerned, and Asa put out tea and manju for her to eat, but the teacher didn't touch them. 'They're not poisoned,' Asa pleaded, crying.

After that, Asa was sent to live with her newly married aunt and uncle on her father's side. Here Asa was given cooking lessons by her aunt, who was a full-time housewife and very proud of it too. Obediently, Asa skimmed the scum off broths, chopped up veggies, sweetened gravies, and turned the flame of the gas down low – but her uncle barely showed the slightest interest in the dishes Asa prepared. Even though he always finished every morsel of his wife's dishes, practically licking the plates. Did they taste so different?

'Is that all you're going to eat?' Asa's aunt would ask, speaking for Asa.

'That's me done. This man is full! Look at my full belly.'

That was a sign for the two women to quickly set about clearing the table.

In the early days, Asa tried to entreat him, time and again, to eat what she had prepared. Sometimes he would yell at her in anger.

The leftovers would be given to the Maltese terrier, the couple's naughty spoilt little puppy, who ate anything – provided that it wasn't Asa who fed it to him.

In her last year of primary school, Asa's mother died. She had been in hospital a long time. As she lay dying, Asa asked if she would like to taste any of her favourite foods for the last time. Her mother asked for sushi. Asa hurried out to get a supermarket pack of sushi. 'Here,' she said, bringing a small ball of pink tuna and rice close to her mother's mouth – but her mother's lips would never open again.

Asa was not able to give her mother anything before she died, not even a single grain of rice.

At this, Asa lost all faith in herself.

Immediately after her mother's death, her aunt and uncle had a baby. A cute little baby boy, who cried, laughed, and drank lots of milk. Asa happily took a hand in the newborn's care. She changed his nappy, she helped bathe him; the only thing she didn't take part in was feeding him. One weekend, while her aunt and uncle were away in town, the baby started to cry and he wouldn't stop. Asa tried to settle him, to no avail, finally deciding that it had to be because he was hungry. Asa went to the kitchen. Defeatedly, she prepared the baby's bottle. Defeatedly, she took the screaming baby on her lap, and defeatedly she put the bottle's teat against his lips. And then the baby started to suck! Asa couldn't believe it! He didn't seem to notice Asa's trembling hand and noisily gulped down every drop.

And then he started to scream again.

'There's more!' Asa leapt up to go to the kitchen. But then on second thought, she sat back down. Stripping off her T-shirt, naked to the waist, she took the baby firmly in her arms and put one of her dry little breasts against his mouth. The baby immediately stopped crying. Making a sucking motion with his lips, he seemed to be deciding whether to latch on (her nipple wouldn't have given him a drop) . . . but the next moment, there was a loud crash. Asa turned, and saw her uncle and aunt. Their heavy shopping bags had slipped out of their hands to the floor.

Asa didn't go near the baby again.

She got through primary school, though with a poor attendance rate. By the time she got to middle school Asa was one of the troublemakers. In her black school bag, she carried not a single school exercise book, but rather sake, cigarettes, some junk food and spare underwear – all shop-lifted from stores around town. Asa took this bag with her as she couch-surfed, staying alternately with other members of her gang. But when she offered the sake and snacks as payment, no one ever accepted them. They just stayed in her bag, forever.

And now, Asa was no longer the class wimp, but the class bully. Still, no matter how domineering she was, the emptiness in her heart remained. One day, Asa made a younger girl she particularly disliked come to the sheds after class. She gave her a head-butt and stripped her of her purse, and then she had the other girls bring her a dead cicada. 'Eat it,' she ordered. The girl refused to open her mouth. Threats, blows – all were no good. The girl kept her mouth closed, stubbornly, fully aware of what would happen if she opened it. Asa gave her several slaps around the top of the head. Then, forcing the other girls to help her, she prised the girl's jaws apart.

'Please,' she begged. 'Eat it.'

In the middle of the school year, at the end of summer, Asa was bundled into her uncle's car and taken to a juvenile correction facility deep in the mountains. Here, adolescents like Asa, who had committed offences, were given instruction in healthy life habits so that they could survive in the outside world after their release. A Buddhist priest, whom the teenagers had to address as Sensei, was her instructor. At first, unable to stand the regimen and the plain food, Asa kept running away. When she was returned, she would have to sit for hours, in silence, in a small room, with no furniture but a desk and two chairs, with the priest sitting opposite her. Thinking about what she'd done.

'I'm going to wait here,' the priest would say, 'till you want to talk.'

A few hours into the silence, there would be a knock, the door would open, and Asa would see the face of the priest's wife. 'Don't tell the others,' she'd say. With a small dry clack, she'd set down a plate of home-made chiffon cake.

As time passed, Asa got used to her life in the correctional centre. After two weeks, her muscles no longer hurt the day after the physical chores – cutting firewood or carrying buckets of water from the well. The numerous classes and activities meant that the days passed in a flash. On weekends she and the other inmates went into town to do work for the community. By the end of her six-month term she really did feel better – stronger, in mind and body.

If only all the inmates had been like Asa. Sensei and his wife would definitely have had an easier time. The only way some of the youths had ever learned to express themselves was through verbal or physical abuse. There were continual fights. One evening, a fight broke out at dinner. One boy's helping of mackerel was smaller than another's. Voices were raised, things got nasty – they could easily have come to blows. But Asa intervened. Picking up her plate, she positioned herself between the brawling boys.

'Why fight? I'm happy to give you mine.'

There was a second when the boys paused. But then –

'Why would I want your food!' one of them snarled. And he knocked the plate from Asa's hand onto the tatami. Asa ended up getting drawn into the fight, and all three of them were slapped across the face by Sensei, and sent to their rooms.

Late that night Asa cried her heart out.

'Why are you so sad?' Sensei asked.

'Nobody eats the food that I give them.' Asa was sobbing. 'Sensei. Are my hands that unclean?'

Sensei took Asa's tear-soaked hands in his own. He turned them over, looked at her palms, and examined them closely. Then he looked up and into her eyes.

'Just the opposite. Your hands are pure. Pure and beautiful.'

And in a moment, Asa fell in love.

And now Asa started to put her very soul into her tasks. She cut twice as much wood as the other teenagers, she volunteered for extra cleaning and laundry duties, she thought up all sorts of good deeds to do in the nearby village, persuading Sensei to give permission to her and the other juvenile offenders. When the elderly residents in a care home refused to take the hot sweet azuki soup she made for them, she pretended she didn't care. And when none of the little kids in the village even looked at the big pile of mochi she had produced after a charity-driven mochi-pounding competition held at the local temple, she was sad, but not devastated. Being in love meant that she felt strong. One day, sent by the priest's wife on a shopping trip, she secretly spent the few pennies she had saved on a chocolate heart.

In early February, when she and the priest were alone in the little room for introspection, she took the chocolate heart from her pocket, and held it out.

'I know it's a little early for this, but . . .'

'For me?'

'Yes. I know you like chocolate. Please, eat it.'

'Ah, that's sweet of you!' said Sensei, and he smiled. But he made no move to take it from her hands.

Sensei had a wife. Asa should have known it was a non-starter. She stared at her hands. At her pure and beautiful hands.

One evening, just days before she was due to leave, Asa was putting together her belongings when one of the other inmates she'd lived with for close to half a year came to her with a proposal. 'Hey, Asa, when we get free time this weekend, let's see if we can go snowboarding! Before you go.'

Two days later, Asa and her companions all

boarded a bus at the local train station and headed for a neighbouring village that had some ski runs. When they arrived at the top of the ski slope, her friends all shot off on their snowboards, one after the other, leaving Asa behind. A newcomer to snowboarding, she descended the slope an inch at a time, not daring to look up. A little way down, she lost control. She tried her utmost to get the board to follow a straight line, but it refused to do what she wanted, and she veered off, then started to fly downhill. Terrified, she closed her eyes, and the next thing she knew she had gone off the ski run, and was racing down a forested mountain-side.

Asa only stopped when she slammed straight into a tree.

She hit her head and lost consciousness. When she came to, everything around her was dark.

She tried to raise herself, but a terrible pain shot through the middle of her body. She had clearly broken some bones. There she lay, quite still, for as long as she could, but then she sensed the presence of some sort of animal nearby. Was it a fox? Maybe a tanuki? If it was a bear, it might eat her up . . . Lying there on her back, Asa raised her head just very slightly, and peered towards her feet. She spotted two glittering eyes quite low to the ground. Probably not a bear. Discovering she could still move one arm, she brought it up to her breast pocket, and pulled out a chocolate – the chocolate heart that Sensei had refused to take. Using her teeth to rip open the packet, she held it out to the animal.

'Come, little one. Eat.'

The animal padded softly over the snow.

'Don't be scared. Eat.'

If she was not mistaken, it was a tanuki. It sniffed at the chocolate, and then, apparently not hungry, turned and padded away.

The forest rang with Asa's laughter.

AHAHA. AHA HA HA HA. She opened her mouth wide, the tears streaming. She beat the nearby plants and bushes with her fist.

'Nobody has ever accepted any of my food!'

And she laughed on and on.

'Why? Somebody tell me! Why?'

Just then something cold and wet landed on her cheek.

Maybe it was a lump of snow, fallen from the branch of a tree? Though from the sweet smell and the watery liquid on her cheek it might be some kind of fruit.

Splosh. This time it fell right onto her eyelids. Hesitantly, Asa licked the juice that spattered over her face. It tasted sweet too. It was a taste she knew. But she couldn't remember what it was. She patted the ground around her head and put the fruit she found into her mouth. It was delicious. It had seeds.

The next thing she knew, the tanuki had come back, and had brought a few companions. Asa lay there listening as they snuffled up the fruit on the ground. If she could be reborn, she thought, watching out of the corner of her eye, she would like to be reborn as a tree. A persimmon tree, a peach tree, an apple tree, a tangerine tree, a fig tree, a loquat tree, a cherry tree . . . She would have sweet fruit growing from every limb, and all the animals of the forest would come and feed from her.

I want to become a tree. Let me become a tree. As her consciousness gradually faded, this was the phrase she repeated to herself, until finally she breathed her last.

When she opened her eyes again, she realised that her wish had come true, and she was now a tree.

Asa the girl who had turned into a tree hadn't any idea of where she was, nor how she had come to be there. Looking about, all she saw was count-less other trees, just like her, growing in the forest, but that gave her no clue at all.

After some time, a lone human being came stumbling along and, a few feet away from her, collapsed. 'I need food,' he said. He lay there in the snow for a long time, without even twitching. Eventually he heaved himself up, and stumbled away eastward through the forest.

Asa watched him go, feeling terrible. She had not been able to offer him a single thing.

If only she'd been an apple tree, or a peach tree, or a mikan tree! How happy she might have been!

Sadly, Asa had turned into a cedar tree. She would never have any sweet fruit to give.

Sometime even later, Asa was felled. Along with all the trees that had been growing around her in the forest, she was loaded onto a truck, and then, her bark and branches exposed to the rough winds, she was transported to a grey-brown factory. There, she was cut up into sections by an enormous rotating blade, and cut up again, this time into smaller pieces, all the while looking on in blank amazement. She was then loaded onto a conveyor belt to be taken to a drying room, and from there transferred onto another belt and transported somewhere else, and finally, before she knew it, inserted into a little transparent sleeve. Not one week had passed since she had been cut down, but she was now a pair of disposable chopsticks.

Next, Asa the girl who had turned into a pair of chopsticks had to be delivered. She was loaded into one truck, then another, and countless more, and eventually she ended up in a drawer beneath the cash register of a convenience store, where for three days she was left just lying there. But on the fourth day, she was fished out and tossed into a plastic carrier bag with a Styrofoam bowl of instant ramen noodles, a makunouchi bento, a can of beer and a pack of tofu. After five minutes of being swung along in the carrier bag, she reached her final destination. A dilapidated old house, its walls overgrown with ivy.

'Hi! I'm back!' she heard.

In this house there lived a young man and a skeleton. The young man was the person who had brought Asa home. The skeleton was a very thin old man – the young man's father.

'Dad. Let's eat.'

The two men sat opposite each other, in a grimy kitchen. The young man filled his cup with mugicha, and his father started chugging back the beer, though it was still early in the day, occasionally pecking with his chopsticks at the block of chilled tofu.

The young man urged his father to eat.

The father picked out a little sausage, and put it with some tofu in a saucer.

'Is that all you're going to take?' the son asked him. The father laid his chopsticks down after taking a small bite.

'You're really finished? Is that all you want?'

'That's me done. This man is full! Look at my full belly.'

The young man sighed, and pulled the plastic container nearer. 'Well, then, I'll have what you've left.' And he ripped open Asa's cellophane wrapper.

In an instant, air filled every cell of Asa's being. Joyfully, deeply, she breathed it in.

The young man grasped Asa by the arms and split her in two. Snap! What a pleasurable sound. A sign that now it would all begin. Asa knew what to do next without even having to be told. Taking a deep breath, she spread her arms wide, and plunged them straight into the warm white rice. Gathering a good heap of it, she heard the young man release a cry of joy as he opened his mouth. Asa let out a cry too, as she dived straight in.

He ate it!

When she came back out, the next thing she reached for was the piece of deep-fried chicken. That too he accepted, taking it straight from her hands, and guzzling it down.

And now the young man proceeded to use Asa to scarf down his food, barely bothering to chew, occasionally pausing for a gulp of tea, but then immediately opening his mouth to shovel in more. Asa found herself jumping into the rice again and again. She did her best to minister to his every need, cleansing his palate with shreds of pickled cabbage, encouraging him with dabs at the salt and sesame seasoning to eat the rice along with the savoury sides so that everything could be finished together. When finally she scraped together the last few grains of rice on the bottom of the plastic box, the tears were falling from her eyes.

'That was delicious!' The young man placed his hands firmly together over his chest, expressing his gratitude.

He wasn't talking to anyone else. The father had

already left the table. No one had ever thanked her like this before.

Next, the young man picked up the plastic carrier bag and quickly tossed in the bento box, the carton for the chilled tofu and the cellophane wrapper. Then he reached for her, and picked her up. Asa readied herself to be chucked in the bag along with the rubbish – she would just let herself fall in, she wouldn't make a fuss . . . She was so grateful. But then the young man did something she didn't expect at all. He put her straight into his glass. Pushing his chair back from the table, he took her, standing upright, to the kitchen sink. The next thing she knew, she was being wiped all over with a soapy sponge, then rinsed in a stream of water and inserted into the little basket on the draining board.

That evening at dinnertime, Asa scooped a bowl of ramen noodles into the young man's mouth.

The young man sucked down the thick curled noodles, swallowing them whole, so fast that he almost choked. 'Don't rush,' Asa told him. Once the meal was finished, she again received a rinsing in the sink, and was then deposited in the draining basket.

So many times, Asa told herself this meal was sure to be her last. Surely this time he was going to get rid of her. But every time, he rinsed her clean and put her in the basket to dry. A few hours later he took her out again.

The face the young man would make as the food she held up went into his mouth was the very picture of joy. Asa would enter his mouth deeply, going right up to her shoulders, sometimes right up to her hips. The moment she slid back out through his lips was so exciting she would never fail to get goose bumps. On the odd occasion, she would also attend to the young man's father. He had lost so many of his teeth, she would have to hold up much smaller portions of rice, and tear any meat she was going to give him into tiny pieces, on a separate saucer. With the young man, she would get wet all over, every time. But with the father, whose mouth was parched of saliva, she hardly got wet at all. The tips of her fingers would just get very slightly moist.

One day it dawned on her that she hadn't fed the father for a while. And not long afterwards, she learned that the old man had died. All that time she had been feeding him, he had been unwell.

The young man took it badly, and became terribly sad.

'You've got to eat!' Asa told him. 'Now more than ever.'

Once the first seven days of mourning were over, the young man set off to the convenience store to buy some food.

That evening, with Asa's help, he sank his teeth into a deep-fried chicken cutlet, and then bowed his head.

'Does that taste good?' Asa asked.

Three months passed, and the young man had clearly regained his hearty appetite. Every morning, after a brief pause to pray in front of the plain wood marker inscribed with his father's Buddhist name, he would use Asa to quickly rake up into his mouth a healthy breakfast of raw egg cracked over a bowl of cooked rice.

One day, the young man began trying to tidy up the house. She had never seen him do anything like this when his father had been alive. He wiped the window panes and the table top with a damp towel, he swept up the dust that had gathered in the corridors with a broom, he even washed the sheets. He was working flat out. Asa began to get anxious. What on earth could have happened?

All became clear the very next day: the young man had found himself a girlfriend.

The girlfriend, whose name appeared to be Miyuki-chan, was a slender young woman with long brown hair that reached down to her waist. Standing in the draining basket, Asa strained to hear the conversation between the young man and the girlfriend, heart pounding. They seemed to have got to know each other in a particular establishment in town. The girlfriend worked there and the young man was her customer. The work took a great toll on her body. The young man was trying to persuade her to give it up.

'I'll go out and work for the two of us.'

'You will?'

'I promise. I'll get a job.'

'You mean, we're going to . . .'

'Yes! Let's get married!'

They decided to move in together. He would go to live in the apartment she owned.

His girlfriend started coming to the house regularly to help him pack up his possessions.

'Let's tidy this mess up!' she would say.

And she would pull back her brown hair, roll up her sleeves, and go about picking things up and tossing them into a big rubbish bag.

'I can't believe you've got so much junk . . . !'

The young man would laugh, embarrassed. He'd watch her with a look suggesting he wanted her to stop, but perhaps because he was already a little scared, he said nothing.

One day, the girlfriend picked up Asa, who was still hiding amongst the cutlery in the draining basket, and threw her in the bag.

'Oh. I want those.'

'Hm?'

'What did you just throw away?'

'I don't know what you mean . . .'

'You just threw something in that bag. What was it?'

'You mean this?' The girlfriend drew one half of Asa out, holding her in her fingertips.

'Put those back where you found them.'

'What?' A frown appeared on the girl's face. 'Do you really want these?'

'Yeah. They can stay,' the young man said.

'Why?' the girl insisted.

'I just don't want to let them go. Leave them.'

'Do you use them?'

'I do.'

'Oh, come on. They're a pair of disposable chopsticks. It's dirty to use them again and again. I've been meaning to tell you to stop being so stingy.'

'Huh? They're still perfectly useable. And to you they might not be anything, but to me they're special. Can you not see that?'

'Special? Special in what way?'

'I don't know. Just . . .'

'Well, I'm going to throw them away.'

'Hey!'

'There. I've done it.'

'You idiot!'

The girl gave a short high-pitched scream. 'That hurts! Ow!'

'Give them back. Now.'

'You're hurting me!'

The young man snatched back the rubbish bag. The girlfriend left the house in tears. And that was the last they ever saw of her.

The young man resumed his previous way of life. He went back to Asa – and to using her to get his meals into his mouth.

Despite his declaration that he would go out and get a job, once his girlfriend left him the young man no longer needed to be in gainful employ-ment. He could go to sleep when he wanted, get up when he wanted. He could spend his time exactly as he pleased. He could watch TV, he could go to

the convenience store . . . or he could go back to
bed.

Oh, please let this way of life continue – forever . . .
Such was Asa's prayer, gazing up at him, as he used
her to stuff his mouth with rice.

And for many years their life did continue like
this, quite peacefully, with nary a worry.

But one day a group of people carrying some heavy
pieces of equipment turned up at the house. The
first visit from outsiders since the split with the
girlfriend. One of these visitors Asa recognised.
He was a comedian in a TV show.

The comedian addressed the young man as
Otōsan – Dad.

'Otōsan! The first step is to separate out the
things you need from the things you can dispose
of!'

'Otōsan! Don't start reading your diary. We've
got a job to do!'

'Otōsan, come on, lend us a hand! Oh, look! A

Peko-chan doll! What an amazing find! Where did you pick this up?'

'Otōsan, where have you disappeared off to? Finally, we get to see the tatami! Camera crew, can you get a shot?'

And the comedian walked through the house with a bin bag in one hand, tossing things in with the other, just like the man's ex-girlfriend had done. Each time he put something in, the young man snatched the bag back, peered in, and picked it out again. 'Don't touch that. I'm using that. I'd rather you didn't go deeper inside the house.'

Eventually, the comedian started to lose patience. The tone he adopted to talk to the young man became more haranguing.

'Otōsan! Quit saying that! Don't you see, I am doing this for you!'

And he would grab the bag back, and barge on. The camera crew entered the kitchen. A foul smell hit them in the face.

The young man followed, begging them to stop, trying to clutch at their shoulders, but he was shoved aside. First to go were the saucepans and the dishes from the piles of objects that lay all over the draining board. Then, the comedian donned some work gloves, and grabbed a fistful of the chopsticks standing in the basket. In amongst these was Asa.

'Not those!' The young man lunged forward, and bit him on the arm.

'Whoa! Jeez! What do you think you're doing!'

'Put those back.'

'Oh, come on now!'

'Put them back!'

'Get off! Get off me!' the comedian shouted, elbowing him off. The young man was knocked back, and slithered down to lie in a heap on the floor, whacking his head on the refrigerator.

'Somebody call an ambulance!' In a few minutes there was the sound of a siren, and the man was taken away to hospital.

Inside the house, now empty of people (since the crew packed up and left), the air was abuzz.

'This is worrisome . . .'

'Hope he'll be okay . . .'

'That was a nasty bang . . .'

'It was his head, I'm sure!'

'Let's hope he survives . . .'

'That comedian seems OK on TV but in real life he's a bully!'

The voices were of Asa's companions. Because in addition to Asa the girl who had turned into a pair of chopsticks, there was Mana the girl who had turned into a pillow, Sho the boy who had turned into a doorknob, Yuta the boy who had turned into a quilt, Kaori the girl who had turned into a blanket, Michiru the girl who had turned into a rock, Noriko the girl who had turned into a clothes hanger, Yoshio the boy who had turned into a Peko-chan doll, Akie the girl who had turned into a knapsack, Soichiro the boy who had turned into a potted cactus, and countless others besides. Each of them had in one way or another undergone some painful experience very similar to Asa's, mostly in their childhood. They had all long ago left this world.

The young man treated them all so carefully, like they were the most precious things in his life.

Please be unharmed. Don't die . . . Asa repeated this prayer the whole night.

The next morning, the young man came home with his head in a bandage. They'd all worried about the amount of blood he had lost but in hospital apparently all he had needed was some stitches to the wound. The TV filming was abandoned, and all the objects of the house resumed their peaceful, undisturbed existence.

'Here, have some food,' Asa would say as she held out a morsel, and the young man would happily accept it.

'Are you nice and warm?' Yuta the boy who had turned into a quilt would hug the man around the shoulders.

'Isn't this cosy!' Kaori the girl who had turned into a blanket would murmur, and she would draw herself closely around his hips.

Sho the boy who had turned into a doorknob would shake hands with the young man every day.

Noriko the girl who had turned into a hanger would drape herself in the young man's clothes.

Akie the girl who had turned into a knapsack would ride around clinging to his back.

And Yoshio the boy who had turned into a Peko-chan doll would get him to give her a pat on the very top of her head.

Now, they were going to be able to live happily ever after.

But not long after the incident with the camera crew, they heard the door chime again. This time the person who visited was an official from the municipal government. The young man listened till the official had said what he had to say, but the man came again and again, and by the third visit, sensing danger, the young man grew agitated, and jostled him out of the house. The officer came again, now with several other people in tow. The young man shouted at them and sprayed them with water from the hose, and threatened to do worse. He was doing everything he could to protect Asa and her companions.

Eventually, the young man received a letter through the slot in the door. It was an official notice telling him he had to clean his house, or he would face eviction.

Yuta had no idea what an eviction order was. Asa did her best to explain. All the possessions in the house were furious at the cold-heartedness of the municipal government, and they all wept in sadness. It would be better to die than to be separated from the young man, Asa sobbed. And everyone else was of the same opinion.

It was deep in the night. Asa and her companions were quietly urging Chika the girl who had turned into a reading lamp to go through with the plan they had all agreed on.

'Come on, go for it!'

'Just one more push and you're there!'

'Take a breather and try again!'

'You can do it!'

On a shelf immediately above Chika, Akira the boy who had turned into a pocket-sized book waited, with his little pages open and at the ready.

With her pals urging her on, Chika took another big breath and concentrated on getting as hot as she possibly could, pushing and pushing, making the bright red shade on her head glow. And then . . . YES! The paper-thin glass of her bulb split, and a tiny spark jumped onto Akira, creating a little flame that then became a fire. The orange flames melted Yoshio the boy who had turned into a Peko-chan doll, and flickered around Akie the girl who had turned into a knapsack, and Soichiro the boy who had turned into a potted cactus, and then whipped about the room, setting fire to the curtains, the wardrobe and the paper sliding doors. The windows of the bedroom shattered, and with a loud cracking sound the ceiling fell in. The young man, wrapped in the arms of Yuta the boy who had turned into a quilt, was fast asleep, snoring, but he was soon engulfed in flames. Blown by the wind, showers of sparks from the flames poured down into the basket on the draining board in the kitchen. Asa's once pure and beautiful hands were now covered with mould, the grime reaching deep down inside her nails. Raising aloft those dirt-blacked hands, Asa let herself be enveloped in a pillar of fire.

NAMI,
WHO WANTED
TO GET HIT
(AND EVENTUALLY
SUCCEEDED)

Nami's daycare centre was easy to pick out because it had a triangular-shaped red roof. The big playground had a giraffe slide, a crocodile see-saw, big toys spinning round on a revolving circular base, and lots of trees – a sawtooth oak, a cherry tree, a crape myrtle – as well as a shed for a goat and a chicken run.

One autumn day when Nami was just five years old she was having fun collecting acorns under the sawtooth oak along with her classmates. The young woman who was Nami's classroom teacher, the children's beloved Maki sensei, was in the playground with them, and each time a child came and showed her an acorn, she would praise them, smile, and pat them on the head. But then a fight broke out, right there in the playground, two boys yelling and flinging their acorns at each other, and it kept going, despite Maki sensei's attempts to break it up. Milk the goat poked its head out of its shed, and – what bad luck! – an acorn hit it right in the face. With a little bleat it retreated, at which Maki sensei, normally so placid, became infuriated.

'Just stop it, dammit!' she yelled.

At this, the headteacher came out into the playground. (A middle-aged man had suddenly emerged in his slip-on sandals. Maki was addressing him as headteacher, so, Nami thought, that's what he must be.) He stood there, arms folded, listening to what Maki sensei reported. Then he turned to the children and yelled.

'Stop playing! Get into a line!'

All of the kids formed a straight line in front of the crocodile see-saw, and the headteacher went from one child to the next, confiscating their collections, insisting they give up not only the acorns they held in their hands, but ones they had stored in their pockets. He put all of their acorns into the little red bucket from the sand box.

'So this is all of them?'

Then the headteacher slowly picked up one of the acorns in the bucket, and, facing one of the boys who'd been in the fight, hurled it at him.

'Ouch!'

The man picked out another acorn, and flung it at the other boy.

'Ouch!'

And the two little boys started to sob, wailing loudly and piteously.

'Well, now you'll be able to appreciate the kind of pain that Milk experienced,' the headteacher said. 'Do you get it? That's what you did to Milk!'

All the children ducked their heads, Nami along with the rest.

'I don't believe you have understood.' The head-teacher shook his head slowly. 'You haven't understood a single thing. The pain that animal felt, and the fear. I think we only understand what pain is once we've felt it ourselves!'

He picked another acorn out of the bucket.

'This is the kind of pain that Milk felt. Here, let me show you.' And with that he took aim at another child and threw it in her face. The child immediately started wailing.

'Do you get it now?' The headteacher stuck his hand into the bucket.

And so he went on, calmly and methodically, as if he were going down an assembly line.

'Now do you get it?' the headteacher repeated, throwing acorns in each child's face. One by one, each child burst into tears. After they'd burst into tears, each child rushed to Maki sensei for consolation. Maki sensei wiped the tears of each child with her hankie, patted their head twice, telling them it would be all right, and sent them inside with a gentle push between the shoulder blades. 'Go back to class, and wait quietly like a good child.'

And one by one the kids went back inside.

But Nami didn't. She remained in the playground. Because no matter how many acorns the headteacher threw at her, they all just whizzed past her.

'Hey. Don't move out of the way!' The headteacher was reaching the end of his tether, and had a furious expression on his face. 'Stay still!'

Nami was so terrified that she started to run.

'I told you, dammit, not to move!'

The next thing Nami knew, she was running round and round the playground with the headteacher hard on her heels. He was coming after her, with the bucket full of acorns.

'Wait! Dammit!'

The headteacher must have thrown twenty or thirty acorns. But every single one whizzed straight past Nami's head, or zipped past her body, ricocheting off the walls and the roof of the shed. After a while, the headteacher was too out of breath to shout. He just grabbed any acorn he saw lying on the ground, and lobbed it.

On and on the acorn attack went, with no sign of any let-up. But while she was running round and round, Nami suddenly heard someone calling her using her nickname: 'Nana-chan!' It was coming from somewhere above.

Looking up, she saw all her classmates hanging out the first-floor windows. They were all looking at her, waving their arms.

'Don't give up, Nana-chan!'

'Nana-chan, don't give up!'

'Nana-chan, run your fastest!'

'Don't give up, Nana-chan!'

'Nana-chan, come on!'

'Don't give up!'

'You can do it, Nana-chan!'

It didn't escape her notice that each one of her cheering friends was clutching a little object in their hand, which Nami recognised in a second. A cute little cracker, in the shape of an animal – a raccoon, cat, lion, pigeon, a parrot, a horse, a turtle, a tapir. Along with the cracker, each child held a little beaker with a lid and straw. Maki sensei had filled all of their beakers with chilled milk.

'Don't give up, Nana-chan!'

'Nana-chan, don't give up!'

Wait. When had it become breaktime? Why had no one told her?

All of her friends were looking at her, cheering her on, taking bites from their crackers and sips from their milk. 'Don't give up, Nana-chan! Nana-chan, don't give up!'

Somebody must have reported what was happening because two police officers came and held the headteacher face down on the ground. At that young and tender age, Nami witnessed someone being restrained and handcuffed. 'Are you okay? Did he hurt you in any way?' the police officer asked.

She shook her head. 'No.' Her classmates had been injured, but she had not. There wasn't a wound to be seen on her body. Not one of the acorns the headteacher had pelted at her had found its mark.

This event became known as the acorn attack, and for a while the neighbourhood buzzed with concern. But by the next spring, no one was talking about it anymore, which was strange, considering what an impact it had had on her. Half a year was all it took for it to be forgotten. With her own memory of the day pushed deep into the back of her mind, the following spring Nami entered primary school.

Nami's daycare centre had been just round the corner from where she lived, but getting to her primary school entailed a forty-minute walk. Her parents ran a vegetable shop, and the family were always preoccupied in the morning, so Nami had to see to her breakfast by herself.

It was a Saturday. Classes were over by midday. Nami did the forty-minute walk home, finished the bread roll she'd left at breakfast, then set out again, heading back to school. She wanted to practise her back flips on the bars in the playground. It was open for pupils to come and go every day except Sundays and national holidays. Today several children were there, all little like Nami. Unlike the swings and the jungle gym, the metal bars were deserted. Nami got down to practice right away. After thirty minutes, she sat down on the edge of the raised flower beds to take a rest when she heard the insistent sound of bells – *dring-driiing! dring-driiing!* – and she saw a group of figures on bicycles pouring in through the school gate. Pausing at the water fountain, they yelled at the little kids.

'Get off the swings and gym, you little runts!'

From their height, they had to be around eleven or twelve. It was against the rules to enter the playground on your bike, or to hog any of the equipment. During school time a figure of authority would run out of the staffroom.

'Get off the swings! What's wrong with you, idiots!'

Seeing all the other children making a dash for the school gate made Nami stand up to go too. As she ran past the boys, she heard a shout.

'Hey! Where are you going!'

She paused, looked back, and saw one of the boys lob something. A spherical object the size of a baseball and orange in colour. Over Nami's head it sailed, to hit the head of a girl just a foot or so in front of her. With a loud splat it broke. The girl gave a short high-pitched scream. In a second, her whole head was soaking wet.

It was a 'water balloon', an origami cube made to hold water.

'Yess! I got her!'

A second water balloon, of blue paper, was

lobbed, then a third. The second hit a boy standing to Nami's left, on the shoulder, releasing its contents, while the third, a pink one, hit the stomach of a girl standing to Nami's right. The entire school playground resounded with the noise of water balloons splattering, and the screams of victims. At the water fountain, balloons were busily being produced for the next round. 'Kyaa! Ah – it's cold! Ouch!' Were there no adults to come and rescue them? Not a sign of any teacher could be seen in the ground-floor staffroom windows. Drenched boys and girls dashed out of the school gate, sobbing, scattering in different directions. Nami dashed away too. Behind her, the water-balloon bullies chased her on their bikes. They caught up right away, and the balloons came thick and fast.

'Take this!' A flying object whizzed past her and burst against an electricity pole just in front of her. 'And this!' Another boy took his hands off his handlebars, and lobbed two water balloons at the same time. The first exploded directly at her feet, the second hit an election poster on a billboard to her side.

'Dammit! Missed again!' The boy banged the handlebars with his fists.

'Well, let's keep going till we get her!'

And they kept at it, non-stop. Nami had no idea when it would end. Then the boys paused to dunk more balloons in the water fountain, and that gave Nami her chance. She hopped over a low brick wall and cut across the garden of an unfamiliar house. She had meant to head home, but now she had no idea where she was. And fear and tiredness seemed to make her feet unwilling to move as she wanted them to, and any number of times she almost fell.

She was limping along a residential street when she heard someone call.

'Nana-chan.'

It came from somewhere above her. Looking up, she saw a face she knew peering down from a first-floor window.

Oh! she thought to herself. Didn't she know this person . . . ? What was she called again? Only a short while before, she had been there in the playground. At that point the child's face and hair had been soaking wet, hit over and over by the exploding balloons. But now, she seemed to be nice and dry.

'Nana-chan.'

Yes?

'Nana-chan. Don't give up!'

What . . . ?

Just then, the window of the house behind slid open, on the first floor.

And then a window in the house next to that.

'Don't give up.'

'Nana-chan, don't give up.'

'Don't give up.'

'Nana-chan, don't give up.'

'Nana-chan, do your best!'

'Run, run, Nana-chan!'

So Nami started once more to run.

First she ran straight, then she turned left, and then she turned right. But wherever she ran, all along the streets, for as far as the eye could see, one window after another was opening. Poking their heads out of the windows, cheering her along, were all the kids who had been there with her in the playground. Everywhere she looked children were waving at her. Lines and lines of faces. Half an hour before, these children had been fleeing with her out the school gate.

'Don't give up!'

'Nana-chan, don't give up.'

'Keep going. Do your best.'

'Do your best, Nana-chan!'

'Run your fastest!'

So Nana-chan ran as fast as she could. She hid in dog kennels and pushed her body deep into hedge-rows to take cover. As she waited for the bicycle bells to go by, she felt as if she was dead.

When she got home, it was evening. Her family members gave her a glance, and carried on with their tasks. If her clothes or her hair had been drenched, it might have been different, but Nami's hair was nicely dry, and so were her clothes, so on the surface everything seemed quite normal. Just as with the incident of the acorns, Nami had escaped unscathed. Nami thought of this as the water-balloon attack.

*

After this came the dodgeball attack, and the empty-can attack.

The dodgeball attack happened when she was in her third year, which was when she first learned about this game. Two opposing teams of players threw soft rubber balls at each other, and any player who was hit was eliminated. ('I'm dead!' they would yell.) If a player caught a ball thrown at them, the thrower would be out, and an eliminated player on the opposing side could get back in the game ('I'm alive again!'). When only two people were left in the game, everybody on the sidelines would be chanting and clapping: 'Last one standing! Last one standing!' The last one standing was the winner.

Nami was always, without fail, the last one standing. The balls the other children threw flew straight past her, spinning through the air, either over her head or just past her body. Day after day, it would be Nami alone who was left on the court. Darting around, dodging balls, right up until the chimes sounded for the end of breaktime.

The attack in question happened one day during lunchtime, shortly before the summer holiday was due to begin. On this day, the school chimes did not sound. Five minutes into the start of the fifth class, their teacher (Nami had forgotten what she was called) came out.

'Children! The midday break is over!' The hem of her skirt was folded up, maybe because she had taken such big strides.

'I want you all back in the classroom now!'

The teacher ran all around the playground, chivvying the children. Finally she got to a little group who were her next class.

'You too. You can't stay out here. It's arts and handicrafts next.'

'Aw . . . ? But the chimes haven't gone!'

'The system is down today. Today, we have to use our watches.'

Just then, the teacher stopped dead in her tracks and stared.

She was staring straight at Nami, a small figure

standing all alone in the middle of the dodgeball court.

'What's the meaning of this?' The teacher whirled round, then glared at each of the children. 'Were all of you ganging up against this one little child?'

'We weren't! We were playing a game! It was dodgeball – what do you expect?' The children all protested.

'Is it right for you to throw balls at someone just because it's a game? That's more like bullying. Dodgeball is supposed to be a team sport. If one team is way stronger than the other, it's not fair. What's the big idea of everybody ganging up against one person?'

This was a teacher who always overreacted to things, and who never listened to what anyone said. Nami huffed exasperatedly.

'Never mind,' the teacher announced. 'Teacher's going to be on her team now.' And she came and joined Nami on the court.

'You'll be fine now.' The teacher patted her on

the shoulder. 'You others,' she told the rest of the children, 'get over to that side.'

'Now we're even. I'll let you into a secret: I was once an ace handball player, and I can catch and throw like a pro. Okay! Give it all you've got! Let's have it!'

At first all the children did was gape at their teacher standing with her arms up in a weird pose, but gradually curiosity got the better of them, and they came back onto the court. Finally all of them had returned, and a new game between teacher and class got underway.

The teacher was indeed quite the athlete. Every ball thrown at her, high or low, she caught, throwing it back to the thrower before her feet had even reached the ground. The other team were eliminated in a few seconds, struck on the chest, the legs, and all of them gathered on the sidelines and complained. 'This is no fun! Teacher, what about our drawing class!'

'How about this?' The teacher leapt into the air to catch a ball, hurling it straight back. 'Any child I hit gets to leave and go back to the classroom!'

'Yippee!' The child she'd hit ran off happily. The teacher hit another child, then two more. In just a few moments, not a single player on the other side remained.

'Well, that's disappointing,' the teacher muttered, staring at the empty court. Then slowly she turned around, and saw Nami. Up till now, Nami had been hiding behind her.

The teacher looked at her and grinned. She readied herself to throw the ball.

'Last one standing,' she said.

But weren't they meant to be on the same team? Involuntarily, Nami broke into a run. She ran over the lines marking out the court, and sprinted straight across the school grounds.

'Get back here!' the teacher yelled, running after her, ball in hand.

This was not dodgeball. It was now, clearly, something else.

'I said get back here!' The teacher hurled a strong fast ball. It skimmed straight past Nami and landed by the gymnasium shed. The teacher sprinted over, picked it up, and threw it at Nami again.

'Wait! I said stop!'

Nami fled. Even when she fell, she got straight back up and continued to run.

As she ran, panting, high above her head she became conscious of some objects joggling in the air. They had been there for some time. What could they be? Nami directed her eyes upward.

Origami paper? Being used for what? Nami tried to focus.

What she saw were letters, letters that formed words.

K̲E̲E̲P̲ G̲O̲I̲N̲G̲ D̲O̲N̲'T̲ G̲I̲V̲E̲ U̲P̲

Sheets of paper, each with one letter written on them, were stuck against the windows of the first-floor classroom.

The kids had used the squares of paper prepared for their arts and crafts class to write their message with their pencils and pens. Each of the letters on the sheets of paper was in a different style and size.

The sheets themselves were of various colours – pink, yellow, red, green, purple . . . DO YOUR BEST DON'T GIVE UP, she read, in a multicoloured array.

All of a sudden the sheets of paper fluttered over, to show their reverse side. Now what the letters said was:

NANA-CHAN KEEP GOING

A sob left Nami's mouth.

DO YOUR BEST NANA-CHAN KEEP GOING NANA-CHAN QUICKLY QUICKLY COME ON DON'T GIVE UP

Nami had yet to understand what these words really meant.

After this, the teacher managed to twist her ankle and fall, and had to be driven to hospital by the deputy head, where she was diagnosed with a compound fracture. Nobody knew if she'd given up her job for good, but she was never seen on the premises ever again.

For the record, not one of the balls thrown by that teacher actually hit their mark. Nami remained unscathed.

And that was the dodgeball attack.

After this, nobody was allowed to play dodgeball at that school. The pupils, especially the older ones, were all outraged, and they directed their anger at Nami. 'It's all your fault we're not allowed to play it anymore,' they would say accusingly. From then on, practically every day, she would find insect carcasses and dog excrement deposited in her shoe locker.

Nami gradually started not going into school at all.

On days when she missed school, Nami would slip out of the house and spend the hours at the top of a hill known in her neighbourhood as the 'mountain'. This was where she and her parents used to come when she was child, to look out over the town cemetery after their annual visits to the family grave at Obon. The three of them would seat themselves on the single wooden bench on the brow of the hill, and munch on onigiri.

When she was skipping school, Nami passed the time sucking on boiled sweets and reading manga, which she brought with her from home.

And it was here that she got to know Nunotaro.

There was not a single person in town, Nami included, who didn't know of Nunotaro, an old man who collected recyclable cans. Everyone had grown so used to seeing him roaming around with a huge thick refuse sack as tall as himself slung over his back. He was like part of the landscape. Some said that Nunotaro had no home, others that he was the heir of a wealthy landowner. Another story claimed that he had once killed a child. It was also said that he gave all the money that he earned from recycling cans to UNICEF.

Nami was sitting on the bench, drinking from a can of juice, when Nunotaro came up behind her.

'Little girl.' He gave her shoulder a poke. She looked round and saw him.

'When you've finished drinking, give me your can.'

Nami nodded, though she was startled. With a big heave-ho, Nunotaro pulled his big bag off his shoulders and set it down on the ground, and then sat cross-legged on the grass. He wiped the sweat off his face with a dirty sleeve, and took out a single crumpled cigarette from deep in his shirt pocket and lit it with a match.

She could see that the bag was barely half full. The old man met Nami's gaze, a little embarrassed. 'My work day has just started.'

Nami acknowledged him politely.

At which point Nunotaro shot her a grin. He had a single, long, black jagged tooth hanging down from his upper gum.

Nami swiftly finished up her drink. When she held the empty can out, Nunotaro took it with his black fingers. 'Thank you for your continued patronage.'

Nami started making a point of bringing a can of orange juice with her when she went to the mountain. Nunotaro didn't always show up, it depended on circumstance, but on days when he didn't, she would place the empty can on the seat of the bench. The next day, when she went up to look, the can would have been collected.

If she couldn't afford to buy a can of juice, she would take an empty vegetable tin, or an empty sake can, which she found by rummaging around in her family's rubbish. The instant she handed Nunotaro an empty can, Nami would get a very strange feeling. That was because Nunotaro would say what he always did, 'Thank you for your continued patronage,' and without fail she would get a glimpse of his long, black, pointed tooth.

One day, yet another day when she was skipping school, Nami set off for the mountain with no empty can in her hands. She'd had no money to buy one from the shop, and she hadn't managed to find one in the family rubbish bins. As she walked, Nami kept glancing all about her, hoping to see a discarded can on the roadside. But cans were not easily found. Not in the rubbish bins in the park, nor in the ditches by the side of the road, nor even in the little tubs placed right by the automated vending machines. She looked and she looked, and after an hour she found not a can but a bottle. A small brown glass bottle for an energising vitamin drink – the word 'VITAMIN' on the label. Nami resumed her climb, the little brown bottle in her hand.

Nunotaro was there, as usual not sitting on the bench but cross-legged on the grass, puffing on a cigarette, his big thick refuse sack packed so full it seemed about to split. Clearly, he had scoured the whole town for cans, which was why she hadn't found any. Seeing her, Nunotaro raised a hand. By now the two of them were used to each other.

Nami gave him a little nod by way of a greeting. And she held out the bottle she'd found. Nunotaro stiffened.

'What's that for?' he muttered, in a low voice.

Nami explained. She hadn't come across any cans . . .

Immediately, Nunotaro's expression changed. His dark face turned purple, and he glared straight at her, enraged. Terrified at his sudden transformation, she froze.

'Why would I want a bottle!' Nunotaro yelled. He advanced towards her, the spit spraying from his mouth, repeating the same thing.

Taking a step back in fright, Nami dropped the bottle, which started to roll down the slope. Nunotaro ran, scooped it up, and threw it at Nami. With a whizz, it flew past her head, hit the trunk of a tree, and fell to the ground.

'Why would I want a bottle?! A bottle? Why would I want a bottle?'

Nami took to her heels. She ran down the hill. Nunotaro came after her, hurling cans from his sack.

'I don't even want cans! I don't even want cans!'

And he didn't stop chasing her even when they reached the bottom. By now it was mid-afternoon, and up ahead along the road Nami caught sight of a group of school children, her classmates, square satchels strapped to their backs, just leaving through the school gate. A can flung by Nunotaro happened to catch one of the children on the head. With a cry of pain, the child fell to the ground. And now Nunotaro was throwing cans indiscriminately, quickly and with force. 'I don't want anything!' he shouted. One by one, other children were struck down, as his cans caught them on the head or the back. Jumping over the prone bodies, her entire attention focused on getting away, Nami ran and ran, but Nunotaro kept up the chase, can in hand. Nami had no idea when it would all stop, nor where she was running.

On that summer afternoon, her face bright red, her lungs gasping for air, finally, Nami took refuge in a park. Here she hid herself in a low hedge, and kept completely still, and as she did she heard a siren approaching. The siren made two sounds. *Pee-paw, pee-paw*, then *oo-oo, oo-oo*. As the sounds came nearer, Nami thought she might ask for help, so she scrambled up. But with a snap and a rustle, Nunotaro rose from the same hedge, his eyes terrifyingly angry. There was a can in his hand. Nami again started to run.

She fled, running and running without stopping. The dual carriageway, a raised footpath, a Shinto shrine, the park, vegetable fields, rice paddies, the shopping centre, the cinema. Sometimes running, sometimes walking, sometimes hiding, Nami ran and ran. *Keep going, Nami. Keep going. You mustn't stop.*

Finally, Nami came to a huge open car park, with a single car parked in it. And here, by the car, she fell down on the tarmac.

She was exhausted. She could no longer get back up. Nami lay there on her back, put her face against a tyre of the car, and quietly closed her eyes. But immediately, they flew open. Someone was calling her.

'Nana-chan.'

She realised that she had been hearing people calling her name for some time. Raising herself off the ground, Nami gazed up at the sky. Why was it always from above?

'Don't give up.'

'Nana-chan, keep going.'

'Don't give up, Nana-chan!'

'Quickly, Nana-chan!'

In the windows of a tall building that towered over the car park lots of little faces were peering out at her. Everyone peering out was waving. Looking carefully, she saw they were all dressed in pyjamas and all had sticking plasters on their cheeks and foreheads.

Ah, so this car park belonged to a hospital. That's what this tall building was, and all these children were in the wards. All the children that Nunotaro had brought down with his cans an hour before had been brought here, in ambulances. They had been given a check-up by the nurses, and were now all waving at her from the windows of the wards.

Shh! Nami put her fingers to her lips.

Shhhh. Quiet. I don't want Nunotaro to know where I am.

But the voices only grew louder. As if they didn't care.

'Don't give up, keep going.'

'Nana-chan, you can do it.'

'Nana-chan, come on!'

'Faster, faster!'

Shhh. Please. Again Nami begged, gesturing. But then she saw that each of the kids was gripping a little white plastic pot. A single glance was all Nami needed to know that it was the sweet, tangy milk drink she used to love to buy whenever she was taken into the hospital as a child. Her favourite drink in all the world.

'Keep going. Keep going.'

'Nana-chan, don't give up.'

On an impulse, Nami scrambled to her feet. So her classmates had all had their bumps and bruises tended, and were wearing fresh clean pyjamas, and were gulping down that chilled tangy milk drink, sitting there in cool, air-conditioned wards?! She started walking. But as she scanned the hospital looking for its entrance, she saw Nunotaro stumbling towards her.

As soon as he realised it was her, he lunged forward, and flung a can straight at her.

'Don't give up, don't give up.'

'Nana-chan, don't stop.'

'Keep going, keep going.'

'Nana-chan, you can do it.'

But the can clattered to the pavement. A security guard had come up behind Nunotaro and now held him face down on the ground in a wrestling lock.

But Nunotaro was still throwing. He was now throwing with air. Over and over again, Nunotaro tried to grab handfuls of air and throw them at her. And Nami evaded him. She twisted her body, stooped low, and jumped high.

And then she set off running again.

'Don't give up, don't give up.'

'Nana-chan, don't stop.'

'Keep going, keep going.'

'Nana-chan, you can do it.'

And then she twigged. She understood what they meant . . . She stopped, and covering her face she burst into tears.

'Nana-chan, don't give up.'

'Nana-chan, keep going.'

'You can do it, Nana-chan.'

Finally she understood. So that's what they were saying . . . When they cheered her, telling her that she shouldn't give up, she had taken them literally, assuming that's exactly what they meant, not to give up and to hurry and get away. But she had been wrong. What they were really saying, what they actually meant, was that they hoped she would be brought down. You can do it, Nana-chan – you can get brought down.

Nana-chan. Keep going and *get brought down. And then you can come and be one of us.*

Of course. Why had it taken her so long to comprehend?

Nami raised her face and looked up, and as she did so, as if to answer her question, she heard their voices, now echoing loudly all across a gloriously blue sky, cheering her on in unison.

'Don't give up, don't give up.'

'You can do it, Nana-chan.'

'Don't give up, don't give up.'

'Nana-chan, come on!'

Come on, hurry and get hit!
Come over and join us!
Once you're brought down, it'll all be over.
It'll all be over, once you get hit.
Once you're brought down, it'll all be over.

From that moment, Nami became a completely different person. She decided that she would not run away from anything. Not from acorns, not from water balloons, not from rubber dodgeballs, not from empty cans . . . After all, the pain of being brought down was temporary. And it was better than exhaustion. On the other side of that brief moment of pain, there'd be animal crackers, milk, art class, chilled tangy milk, freshly washed pyjamas, friendly waves of the hand, and a place, finally, where she was safe . . . If the other kids had such things, why couldn't she?

She wanted those things. Right now.

An irrepressible desire rose from the depths of her body.

79

And now Nami began a totally different struggle.

The very next day, Nami started to go out on walks. She went anywhere and everywhere. Just staying inside, nothing would come her way. Round and round her town she walked, from morning till evening. The first day, nothing happened to her. The second day too, not a single knock, nor a blow. It was the same thing on the third day. One whole week went by. Nami decided to go to a place where there were lots and lots of people. Getting on the bus, she headed for the biggest park in the town.

The moment she set foot in the park, she got a strong feeling that here, definitely, she'd get hit. In all this space, there seemed to be lots of things flying in the air and lying on the ground – there were balls, there were discarded cans, there were chestnuts, there was rubbish; everywhere she looked there was something. So many things caught her eye she felt quite overwhelmed . . . For Nami, anything, anything, would have done.

Just then, she saw a Frisbee coming towards her.

This was it, she thought. A flying yellow Frisbee, soaring through the air in a long arc, small at first, when it was way off in the distance, but growing bigger as it drew closer. But just when she thought it would fly straight into her, suddenly, a big ball of fur blocked her vision. 'John! Great catch!' she heard. The next moment, both fur and Frisbee sailed out of sight.

A few seconds later her head cleared, and she realised a large and very fluffy dog had intercepted it at the last minute and run off. With the Frisbee in its mouth, it headed back to its owner. 'Good boy, John!' The man caressed the dog's head, tousling its fur. He took back the Frisbee and held up a finger, signalling one more time. Here was her chance. Nami ran after the Frisbee, not to be outdone. This time she was determined, she was definitely going to do it . . . But again, no luck. Dozens of times she tried, but her little leaps couldn't compete with the dog's powerful bounds.

The next thing she tried was a football. A group was having a football game in a corner of the park.

When she ran over and tried to join in, she heard the shrill sound of a whistle: *Phwwwwwhht!* 'Sorry. We're in the middle of the game. Please leave.' She was pulled off the pitch.

Next she tried acorns. A mother and toddler were sitting under a sawtooth oak tree, gathering acorns. Nami joined them, and gave all the acorns she gathered to the little girl. 'Thank you! So we can have all of yours? What do you say, Yui-chan?'

'Fan ku.'

But neither child nor mother seemed to get the urge to toss an acorn at her. Nami found herself wishing for her daycare's headteacher to be there. Unable to wait, Nami decided to show them what to do. She scooped up an acorn lying at her feet, and threw it straight at the toddler's forehead. The toddler started wailing. 'What a horrible girl!' At the sound of the mother's voice, a crowd of people came running over. Nami hastily ran out of the park.

Despite such failures, Nami persisted, going out day after day, visiting one place after another, searching for any opportunity to end up hurt. One time she rushed straight into a group of children kicking a ball about in a park, and tried to join in to get a ball kicked at her. One time she went to a baseball game and waited for a foul ball to hit her in the face. She walked up and down under tower blocks in her neighbourhood, hoping for a plant pot on a balcony to fall and hit her on the head. On nights when a strong wind blew she would wait outside in the street, wishing that a notice-board would whack into her. She also, once or twice, rushed straight out into the road in the hope that she would be hit by an oncoming car. But nothing worked. No ball came close, no notice-board whacked into her, and no plant pot ever fell. Oncoming cars would swerve by her, smashing straight into telegraph poles and walls, coming to a standstill and emitting smoke.

So the days went by, her desire unmet. She left the primary school that she had barely attended, and then, almost before she knew it, she was at middle school.

But it made little difference. All day and every day, she thought of nothing else. She had to get something – anything – to hit her.

One morning, she made an announcement at breakfast that she was actually going to school. Her family were quite surprised – she had let a good two months slip by after the entrance ceremony. The truth was that the previous night she had remembered – at her new school, dodgeball wouldn't be forbidden. She'd be able to play it freely. The whole point of dodgeball was to get hit. All she'd have to do was stand there and not dodge. And of course she wouldn't do that . . . Not when getting hit was her heart's desire. The thought had made it impossible to lie still. She had started to get ready for school in the middle of the night, and left her breakfast untouched.

When Nami walked through the school gates, she was shown to her desk by a woman who told her she was her classroom teacher. Everything was going exactly to plan. All she had to do now was wait for breaktime.

And finally it arrived. Nami stood in the play-ground, but no one came out to play. She waited, a solitary figure, loitering there until it was time for classes to resume.

Nami went to school the following day as well. As soon as the chimes sounded for breaktime she ran out to the playground, but no one came out with her this time either.

On her return to the classroom, she took a fresh look round. All around her sat girls dressed in dark blue uniforms, just like her own. They were all huddled in small groups, and all eating onigiri, chattering away. They exchanged stories about what they'd watched on TV the night before, or boys they had a crush on. A few of them opened up their exercise books and started doing sums or writing out answers.

'Let's play dodgeball!' Nami went round the whole classroom. Everyone she asked scowled, and turned their back. 'Well, how about volleyball? Or basketball?' Anything to get a ball thrown at her . . . During health and PE class, Nami yelled as loudly as she could: 'Pass! Pass!' But nobody did. Nobody let her even touch the ball. And that wasn't all: they also avoided looking her in the eyes, and talking to her. It seemed very much like they were bullying her – the kind of bullying that involved acting as if she didn't exist. There was another child in the class whom the other kids liked to pick on. They would hurl rubbish at her, and dusters. Nami would look at her with envy. If only she could trade places. No one would throw anything at her. There was nothing for anyone to throw at.

She couldn't continue like this. Maybe nothing would ever hit her, ever. For her entire life.

Nami grew desperate with impatience.

When Nami picked up the rubber, it was only because it happened to be lying near her. She grasped the hard little object, feeling it with her fingers, and the next minute she'd tossed it at her own face.

Thwap! The rubber hit her right cheek.

Next she snatched up an automatic pencil, and pointing it at herself, she tossed that. It landed back on top of her desk.

The next object she threw at herself was a ruler. It hit her forehead, producing a light brittle sound – *kawhak!* It bounced off, back down on the desk, with a little *klak!*, then fell to the floor. She threw one thing after another: first a ballpoint pen, then her pencil case, her textbook, her notepad, her dictionary – anything within reach. Her pencil case hit her on the nose – *plap!* Her exercise book hit her on the top of her head – *thunk!* Her notebook hit her straight in the chest – *whhp!* Her English dictionary hit her on the side of her head – *whud!* When not a single item remained on her desktop, Nami started using her own fists. She punched her own cheek. *Whack!* That was the heaviest sound yet.

She was suddenly aware of someone's gaze. The boy next to her was staring at her, his face as white as a sheet. The teacher too was watching her in alarm. What was she doing? This was the middle of a lesson! Quickly she scooped up all the items off the floor, but just before she put them back on her desk, she landed one more punch on her own face. *Whack!* And one more time. *Whack!* One more time. *Whack!* By now there were some sounds of consternation amongst her classmates. All of a sudden, the soft sounds of the notes of an alto recorder reached her ears. And still she punched. MI, FA, SO . . . *Whack! Whack!* MI, FA, SO . . . *Whack! Whack!* Somewhere, it seemed, some of the kids were learning how to play the recorder. It was just as if Nami's punches were providing the beat for what they were playing. MI, FA~, SO, SO~, *Whack!* La, So, MI~, *Whack! Whack!* SO, FA~#, RE, RE, DO, DO, *DOn't give up, DOn't give up, Na na cha n, DOn't give up,* DO, MI, RE, SO, FA~, Mi~ . . . G e t h i t, a n d i t w i l l s o o n b e o v e r . . . I f y o u d o n't g e t h i t, t h i s w i l l a l l g o o n f o r e v e r . . . I t w i l l n e v e r e v e r e n d. *Whack. Whack.*

That's strange, Nami thought. Nothing had changed. Nothing had ended at all.

It was soon after this that somebody decided Nami had to be hospitalised. On the morning she was due to go in, Nami resisted violently. Not one of the adults around her could subdue her. So she was comforted with patience and kind words. Drink this, you must be thirsty with all that shouting. A Coca-Cola was proffered. As soon as she drank it she was seized with an irresistible urge to sleep, and when she woke up she was in hospital.

She was put into a four-person ward, along with three other young women, all in their early twenties, which meant that they could talk down to her. Without any hesitation, each of them introduced themselves, talking at length and in great detail.

'And you? What are you in here for? What's your illness?'

She didn't reply. She wasn't ill.

And that was how she replied – 'I'm not ill!' – when they asked her again. At this, the other three all looked at each other and tittered. There was no way that her life in hospital with such companions was going to be pleasant.

Every activity she engaged in while in hospital was managed. Apart from when she had counselling, Nami made the excuse that she was ill and spent all of her time in bed. Since even at mealtimes she was hidden behind her cubicle curtains, her three companions gradually stopped talking to her. Instead, they started to play spiteful tricks on her. They would throw her belongings into the bin, or say horrible things about her in earshot, or write indecent graffiti on her plastic slippers. Stupid and childish, too stupid to take any notice of, but one day when Nami came back from the toilet to find her bed soaking wet she lost her temper, and in full view of her three colleagues, she spat into each of their drinking mugs in turn.

'What do you think you're doing?' The dumpiest got out of bed, and rushed over to Nami. She raised her fist, right up close to Nami's face. As her fist swung down, Nami involuntarily closed her eyes . . . But nothing happened. She opened them again, carefully. The three of them were laughing and pointing at her.

'Look at her, freaking out . . . !'

Nami grabbed the girl by the front of her shirt and sat her down hard. Down the girl went, and Nami got on top of her. 'Why?' she yelled. Why? Why hadn't she followed through? She had been so close to getting hit!

Nami made a fist with her hand. The girl shrieked.

Whack. And again. *Whack.* Nami was hitting herself, bringing her fist to her own cheek. Time and again. Repeatedly.

Late that night, Nami was called in for a counselling session.

A doctor, a short man with a big head, had asked to speak to her. This doctor was Nami's principal psychiatrist. One afternoon a week, she would go to see him. Nami would be silent, but the doctor would tell her all sorts of information about himself. He would tell her about the movies that he liked, or the books that he read, or memorable incidents that had happened to him on holiday, or times that he had messed up at school. Nami liked to listen to what he told her. If there were a few brief moments that were less pointless in all the days she spent there in that hospital, it was the time she spent in his company.

But now it was midnight. And it wasn't her usual day. The doctor stared at her as she sat there before him. The expression on his face was slightly different from usual.

Mustering up courage, Nami asked: 'Why are you looking at me like that?' The next moment, the doctor stretched out his hand.

And he touched her swollen face gently with his fingers.

'Doesn't this hurt?' he asked, softly.

Nami shook her head.

'It must hurt, surely.'

She shook her head again. And then she realised that he was looking terribly sad.

When had she ever seen such sadness in another human being?

The doctor spoke again.

'Will you tell me why?'

Why what . . . ?

'Tell me the reason why you are compelled to hit yourself.'

'I don't hit myself,' Nami said quickly. 'I'm not hitting myself. I'm just bringing my fist up against myself . . .'

'Hm.' The doctor said this with an air of sadness. 'Why do you feel the need to do that?'

Why? Because who else will, if I don't? And anyway, it doesn't have to be my fist. It can be a ball, or an empty can – anything – just as long as it comes up against me. That's what I want. Something that has an impact. But it doesn't happen. That's why I'm doing it to myself. My fist is the . . . nearest thing I've got. It's convenient, that's all . . .

It was difficult to explain. 'I want something to hit me. I just need that. All I've wanted, for so long now, is for something to hit me . . .'

A little of the strength of her feelings at least seemed to get across to the doctor.

'Why? Why do you want that?'

'Why? Why do you keep asking me "why"?'

'Why do you want that so badly?'

'Well, if I don't, nothing is going to end . . .'

'End? What do you want to end?'

'What do I want to end? Everything.'

The doctor tilted his head a little, then gave a short sigh. No more questions seemed to be coming from him, so now it was Nami's turn. She asked him how long she would have to be in this place before they let her out.

'You'll be let out when you cease beating yourself up.'

But I'm not beating myself up. I told you. She bit back these words. She nodded meekly.

'I understand. I won't beat myself up anymore.'

'Is that true?' The doctor seemed nonplussed.

'I promise,' she said. 'But in return, I want you to bring your fist . . . up against my cheek.' And she pointed to his hand.

The doctor's eyes widened in shock.

'Please.' Nami quickly lowered her head. She had hit herself in the face any number of times, but nothing had ended, at all, for her. Maybe because she was doing it herself.

'Please, doctor, please bring your fist against my face. I think that may do it . . .'

She turned her cheek to him.

The doctor swallowed, audibly.

'Is that what you want? Really?'

'I do.'

The doctor folded his fingers and tucked his thumb over them to make a fist. For a brief moment, he gazed at his hand silently, and then made a jab.

Nami kept her eyes wide open. She wanted to see what was coming.

His hard-looking fist stopped at the surface of her cheek. She felt a short rush of air, along with the sound, then felt a deep, deep disappointment.

'Doctor.' Nami bowed her head. 'Do it again. This time, see it through.' Again the doctor bunched his fingers into a fist. He made a jab, but again, he stopped before contact.

'Doctor.' Nami clung to him. 'Why? Please try, once more! This time, follow through!'

And then, Nami realised something. The doctor

looked extremely tormented. She had never seen anybody look like this in all her life.

Softly, he put his hands on her shoulders. Gently, he lifted her up, and held her face in his hands, resting his fingers lightly on her cheeks.

And, still tormented, he said this:

'How could I do that? How could I hurt such a lovely face. I couldn't. I can't.'

And that was how their relationship began.

Two weeks after they became involved, Nami learned that the doctor was married. But this made no difference to her feelings. In love for the first time, for her, he was the centre of her life.

He told her, over and again, he would leave his wife and marry her. We'll marry on your twentieth birthday – it'll be our wedding anniversary too! That would mean five years of waiting, but that's what it would take to get his wife to agree, he said. Nami believed him. Nami and the doctor had sexual relations in the hospital, any number of times, eluding observation. Nami started taking care of her physical appearance. She washed her face on getting up in the morning, she brushed her teeth, she combed her hair, she applied lip cream to her cracked lips. The doctor told her that he'd prefer it if she were plumper, so she ate well, leaving nothing on her plate, and since he'd forbidden it, she also stopped hitting herself in the face. She started to feel an abatement of that urge that she used to get roiling up inside her, the one she had experienced so many times – that longing to be brought down.

And now the people around her began to suspect something was going on, and they enquired, quite persistently: Has something happened? Nami did not tell them anything. This was because the doctor had told her she absolutely had to keep their relationship secret. And the two of them kept on meeting, and Nami got much better, quickly, and half a year later it was decided that she could be discharged. Round about the same time, Nami found that she was pregnant with the doctor's child.

Nami was unaware for the first few months that she was pregnant. When she put two and two together, she was so far along that she had no choice but to bring the baby into the world. She told the doctor, and he was furious. With angry red eyes, he stared first at her face, and then at her belly, and kept repeating: If you tell anybody about this! You better not! She didn't yet know, but the doctor's wife was the daughter of the director of the hospital, his only child in fact, and the doctor was counting on inheriting his position. The truth was, he'd never had any intention of making Nami his wife.

Nami didn't tell anyone that she was pregnant. She decided not to go back to her family. Instead, she moved to a little one-room apartment belonging, she was told, to a distant relative of the doctor. Here, gazing at her steadily growing belly, Nami spent her time fixing delicacies for him to eat when he visited, or arranging the bits of furniture in her room. She was bored out of her mind, but she still believed that at the end of all of this, she would be married.

The doctor visited two or three times a week. He would bring in provisions, and then lie around on the tatami for a while and have a nap. When he woke up, he would eat whatever Nami had prepared, lie around doing nothing again, then have a proper sleep. In the few minutes before he left, he would address a word or two to the baby in her belly.

'If you're a boy, your name will be Nanao. If you're a girl, you'll be Nanako.' All names that had obvious echoes of her – the mother's – name. Nami would suggest names that had echoes of his name, rather than hers. But this only made him annoyed. 'Don't be stupid.' That was the one thing this doctor wanted to avoid – for the child to be identified with him.

Early one morning on a rainy day in August, Nami gave birth there on the tatami mats in her apartment, with the doctor in attendance. After thirty-two hours of labour, the baby that emerged was a boy. Which meant that he was given the name Nanao.

*

Nanao was a baby that cried constantly. The doctor's visits grew less frequent, he said because the
screaming was too much for him. He started coming twice a week, then once, and some weeks he
didn't come by at all. On weeks when he didn't
show, a huge parcel would be delivered in his stead.
In it was food, drinks in bottles and cans, dried
formula milk, nappies, toilet paper and toothpaste,
and all sorts of other daily necessities, filling it to
bursting. One day she saw a note attached to one
of the nappy bags with his handwriting on it: 'I
can't come and see you for a while.' And with that,
the doctor ceased coming altogether.

And so Nami reverted to how she had been
before. Now that the doctor was no longer with her,
there was no need to clean the apartment, no need
to change her clothes, no need to wash her face, or
make herself look nice at all. With nothing but the
baby's screams in her ears from dawn till night, a
hatred for everything grew in her. She couldn't be
bothered to give the baby milk, or to change his

nappies; she couldn't be bothered to eat or drink herself. At these times, when she felt that there was no hope in anything, frequently she went back on what she'd promised the doctor, and she hit her own cheeks with her fists. Reeling under the heft of the blows she delivered, only when she felt that dull pain was she able to bear the screams of the baby and her sadness at the doctor not being there.

His parcels, however, continued to arrive. Bread, and rice, and instant ramen, and cakes and crackers – including the animal crackers Nami had been fond of as a child. Rather than making proper meals, Nami often just ate these, and she gave them to her son as well, though as yet he still had no teeth. In addition to the food, there were children's books and toys and play-dough, loads and loads of them. But one day, these parcels too suddenly stopped.

One hot day in July, Nami visited the hospital, with her baby. She mentioned the doctor's name at reception, and requested to meet him, only to be told that no person by that name worked there, at which point her mind went blank. It couldn't be true, of course he worked there! She persisted, and then a cleaning lady who happened to be passing by told her quietly what had happened. The doctor had been arrested, on suspicion of child sexual exploit- ation, just two months before, exactly the time the parcels stopped. The case had been settled out of court, the doctor had been released. Nami visited his home address, but he had sold up and left.

Nami lived for seven years with baby Nanao in that apartment. In that room, where gas and elec- tricity, water, all utilities had been cut off, Nanao would cry and cry. He would cry because he was scared of the pitch-black darkness at night, he would cry when he wanted a drink, he would cry when he wanted to eat. And Nami continued to hit herself on the face, in her usual way, with her fists. *Whack, whack.* The sound sometimes made Nanao come running over. He was supposed to be sleep- ing, and yet now he was bawling his eyes out, and clinging to her arm. Crying and sobbing, he would beg her to stop, Nami would push him away, and his head would hit the wall, and he would scream in pain. She took no notice. *Whack!* Tears streaming, Nanao would block his ears.

When Nami tried to run into traffic, Nanao followed her, clinging to her, screaming, 'Don't, don't, Mummy!' When she disregarded the pole at the railway level crossing when it came down before an approaching train, and kept on walking out across the tracks, Nanao ran ahead and spread his arms, saying, 'No, Mummy, no!', crying again. When storms came, and violent winds blew, Nanao would go out to his wandering mother and pull her in. 'Come home, Mummy,' he would say, his face streaming with tears. Nanao was never not crying. One night, late, Nanao asked his mother a question. 'Hey, Mummy, why do you do that? Why do you hit yourself in the face, and try to injure yourself by running into a car on the road, why do you do those things?'

And Nami started to explain why. She started with the acorn attack, and then the water-balloon attack, the dodgeball attack; she told him all about

Nunotaro, and all about how the children urged her not to give up, and then all about what had happened with the doctor who was his father.

Nami's story continued deep into the night, and she was still telling it as the sun rose. At some point, Nanao lost the thread. His mother was using a lot of words that he didn't understand. But Nanao did not stop listening. 'Do you understand now?' she asked him. 'That's what's making me do it.' And, rubbing his eyes, Nanao nodded. 'I understand.'

But telling someone seemed to have done nothing to quieten her need. Day after day after day, Nami went out onto the streets and wandered around. And there behind her, trotting along in women's shoes way too big for him, was Nanao, trying to catch up with her. There was Nami, waiting just outside the baseball ground for a ball to come sailing over to her. There was Nami, out in windy weather spending whole days just wandering around on the streets in the hope that some object blown on the wind would fly into her and knock her flat. And there was Nami, back in her apartment every night, hitting herself in the face, as if in an attempt to work her rage out of herself that way. And Nanao was clinging to her arm, screaming and crying and asking her to stop. The scene was repeated every day, and became a normal part of their life.

Until something happened that brought it all to an abrupt end.

It was the summer when Nanao turned seven. A group of people made an unannounced visit to their home.

Standing at her door, they asked Nami a number of questions. She replied in monosyllables, head nodding, head tilting. Then one of the people looked beyond her, and smilingly beckoned to Nanao, who was inside. He put on his mother's shoes. 'Don't you have your own shoes?' he was asked. Nanao shook his head. As he stepped outside, one of the people, who had gone away briefly, came back, with, as if by magic, a pair of small white plimsolls. When Nanao put them on, his face was like a flower suddenly coming into bloom, searing itself into Nami's memory forever. 'An exact fit, look, a pair of shoes for you . . .' Nami stood there in her doorway, in tears. 'Hey, how about that, Nanao? Your very own shoes. Like Cinderella. Isn't that nice?' But Nanao was looking scared. Now he was being ushered away, a hand pushing him in between his shoulder blades. Nami saw him looking back countless times. The door banged. From the other side of that closed door, she could still hear him crying.

A few days after Nanao was taken away, Nami herself was taken to live in the Azami Lodge, a shelter run by a private support group for women who were poor, unemployed or homeless, and had no other means of recourse. Here, Nami spent her days with other women who were vulnerable and at risk, living under a strict regime, receiving basic vocational training.

Nami had barely attended any school, so she was hardly even literate. The staff did their best to

teach her all they could, patiently and persistently, starting with the basics. She was not the best
of pupils. A woman named Yoneda taught her
manners and common sense. She taught her the
things that children at primary school learned –
numeracy, the stages of her national history, how to
remove ketchup stains, and how to cultivate chives
in pots. One night, Yoneda invited Nami and all
the girls up to the shelter's roof-top patio. Insert-
ing the key into the padlock of the rooftop door,
Yoneda glanced over her shoulder. 'A special treat.'
That night, they all got to watch a show of fireworks. Everyone gazed up with tears in their eyes.
Some women cried recalling times they'd watched
fireworks with a person they loved, others cried
because it was the first time in their lives they'd
seen fireworks. Nami cried because she was thinking about Nanao. She longed to see him. Maybe he
was watching the fireworks too.

Nanao was in fact in another facility run by the
same organisation. It was not far away. It was perfectly possible to go and visit him. All she had to

do was follow procedure and apply for permission.

'The mother is the most important thing in a child's life,' Yoneda would tell her. As if she didn't know it already.

But Nami did not want to visit him. She did not go, not even once. The staff would suggest it, but she shook her head, silently.

She was scared. That he would refuse to see her, that he might accuse the mother who hadn't bought him shoes or sent him to school . . . or even that he might deny she was his mother.

She wasn't a mother. She had long ago lost any right to call herself a mother. She didn't feel ready yet – either to become a mother, or to accept herself as his.

Having taken some classes, Nami set about finding a job. She applied for everything available. Positions in business, sales, admin, reception . . . But not one of these applications went well. Since she seemed not to be at her best when she was among people, Yoneda recommended her for a job at a factory making boxed lunches.

Here she did get hired, but that very same day she was given some news that surprised and confused her. Nanao might be put up for adoption. What? She had never even considered the idea. She had been holding out hope that she might be able to take him back. Everything she had been doing, all the skills she had been acquiring, had been with that in mind.

'But I thought you didn't want him!' Yoneda exclaimed. 'There you have been telling me all this time you didn't feel fit to be his mother. You never visited . . . I assumed you wanted to wash your hands of him. I see! Well, don't take it the wrong way. We have to get the biological mother's consent anyway. We were just positing it as an idea. We'll tell the prospective parents that you've changed your mind.' And then she added, 'Yes, when all is said and done, far better for him to be with his biological mother than a family he doesn't know. Even if they do have lots of money . . . We just wanted to consider his long-term happiness . . .'

Nanao's long-term happiness . . .

Nami told Yoneda that she consented to the adoption after all. Ironically, it may have been the first true act of kindness Nami ever performed for her son.

Once she got the job in the factory, Nami set up home by herself. Her apartment, which she secured with the guarantee of the shelter, was like the one she had lived in with Nanao when he'd been a baby. Stains on the ceiling, holes in the anti-mosquito netting in the windows . . . An image of two storks was painted on the framed, papered doors. Nami thought she could hear Nanao's voice telling her that he was the little bird and she was the big one.

She did not do well at the job she'd worked so hard to find, and within two months she quit. After barely a few hours a call came through from Yoneda, who obviously knew what had happened. Nami assured her that she would look for another job, but only a day later Yoneda called again. Nami gave a vague reply and cut the call, but Yoneda called back. Nami did not pick up. The next day on her return home from a visit to the supermarket she found a note in her mailbox: 'Sorry you weren't home. I'll come by again soon.' From Yoneda.

Without even thinking about it, Nami packed up her meagre belongings and left. That night she slept outside in a public park.

It would only be a matter of time before she was thrown out. She had paid no rent. She didn't want to go back. Who knew when Yoneda might show up at the door. Nami spent the days wandering aimlessly around the town, and the nights sleeping on a bench near the station or in a public park. Any number of times drunks tried to snuggle up to her, and she had to get up and walk here and there, trying to find a safer place to sleep. On nights when a cold wind blew, she would long with all her heart for her bunk bed back at the Azami Lodge. A woman called Shinozuka, forty-two years old, had slept in the bunk above her. *Shinozuka snores like a pig*, Nami had once written on the wall. How dear to her those snores seemed now.

Just once, Nami went back to the shelter. When

she pressed the button on the intercom system on the front door, she caught a brief burst of conversation between Yoneda and the inmates. She hurried away. No way was she going to go back there. That was a place for people who wanted to rebuild their lives. Where could she go now? Was there any place for her?

Nami now simply wandered around. When it began to rain, she took refuge inside a building – it was warm, with a distinct smell. She didn't know it, but the scent was the odour of paper. It was a library. A place she had never been before.

One corner of the library had some soft raised tatami mats on the floor. A reading nook, where parents could read books to their children. Right at that moment she could see a mother reading to her little son, who was sitting in her lap, about a papier-mâché Daruma doll, and at certain points he would start chuckling. When Nami stepped onto the tatami, the mother turned her face away sharply, and the little boy put his hand to his nose. 'What a stink!' Nami made herself small, and went to sit on the other side of the room, where she could lean up against a bookcase.

Sometime later, someone tapped her on the shoulder. A young man with silver spectacles peered into her face.

'Are you all right?'

She had dozed off. The other readers had all left.

'The library's closing,' the young man told her.

She made her way out. She felt strangely light, almost refreshed, perhaps due to sleeping on tatami. Nami headed out onto the already darkened streets.

From that day on, Nami lived according to a new routine. Sleeping in the library by day, and by night up wandering the streets. Night was by far the best time for foraging, and it was also safe. Right by the library was a convenience store where food that had reached its sell-by date would be put out in the collection point at midnight. She would rummage for provisions there, and then head for the centre of town, anywhere with lots of cars and people, where she would stay till dawn. As soon as the sun came up, she would move to a large square immediately behind the library, where she could see the clock tower. As soon as it showed ten, she would enter the building, where she would be able to sleep. At just before five in the afternoon, the silver-spectacled man would come and prod her shoulder.

It was night, a few minutes past midnight. Nami was waiting at the convenience store. The doors opened, and a young man walked out holding a metal wastebasket. Hair dyed blond, jingling gold bangles on his wrists. He lifted the lid of the skip, tipped the contents of the basket into it, replaced the lid, and went back inside. The recycling truck would be there in just a few minutes. Nami tiptoed forward. Suddenly, the doors slid open. The youth thrust out a can of coffee. 'Take this.' Nami was stunned.

'Um . . . er . . .' she muttered.

'Take it. It must be tough living a life like yours . . .'

Nami mumbled an answer, swallowing her

words. She reached forward. The youth had gold jewellery all over him – not only his wrists but his fingers too, and around his neck, and even on his face. Nami had seen him before.

'Nanao?!'

'Huh?'

'. . . You're Nanao! . . . Aren't you?'

'I'm Tomoya.'

'Oh . . . Sorry. I mistook you for someone else . . .'

Nami took the coffee, and the automatic glass door slid shut.

Why would he have been Nanao? He didn't look like Nanao, he wasn't even the same age. And anyway, Nanao would never be found round here. He was living with his adopted family, who had money . . . Nanao . . . I hope you're managing okay . . . living with strangers . . . I hope they're treating you well. I hope they're not abusing or neglecting you. I hope you're not out on the streets, hungry, with nowhere to go . . .

That night she accosted one man after another. Nanao? You're Nanao, aren't you? I know! You are, aren't you?! Nanao! Answer me, please. One of them had his back to her, and she tried to force him to turn round.

When he turned, she saw that he was wearing silver spectacles. He peered at her.

'Are you all right?'

'I need to see Nanao . . .'

'I'm afraid I'm not him . . .'

What was happening . . .

'You were crying out, as you slept. Were you having a bad dream?'

A dream? Slowly she sat up. She was in the library.

All night she had wandered around looking . . . sleeping, very deeply, in her usual spot.

'Sorry to have to tell you. The library's about to close.' The young man unlocked the door.

As she stepped out, keeping her head low, the young man spoke.

'So you are looking for someone.'

Nami paused and looked at him. The young man carried on, his voice soft.

'Someone important.'

Nami nodded. 'Yes.'

He spoke again. 'It'll be all right. You will meet him.'

What could he mean?

'I will . . . ?'

'Absolutely.'

'What do I have to do?'

'You don't have to do anything. As long as you have thoughts in your heart. That's all you need.'

Thoughts?

'So, all I have to do is think of him?'

The young man nodded.

'I'll get to meet him, if I do that?'

'You will. Just wait.'

'I don't have to search?'

The young man placed a hand softly on his breast.

'There's no need to look for him. You have him in your thoughts.' The young man was staring straight at Nami's forehead, at a spot in between her eyebrows. What was he looking at? 'But you should probably try and remain in one place.'

Nami swallowed. The young man narrowed his eyes and smiled. And he repeated: 'You will meet him.'

Somehow she felt encouraged.

'Thank you. I'll try my best . . .'

'Keep a careful lookout. Make sure you don't miss him.'

That night, Nami did not wander. She sat on a single bench in the square, absolutely still, and waited for Nanao to come. She didn't move, not even when drunks came and gave her a hard time and cats pissed on her leg.

Dawn arrived, and Nanao hadn't come. Had that man lied? But wait. He had never said that Nanao would come here. Maybe there was a better place. She should have asked . . . She waited for the clock tower in the square to show ten and then hurried into the library.

Normally she hurried to the reading corner and lay on the floor. Today, she went to the reception desk, to the chief librarian, who had a name tag with his title on his chest. As soon as she entered, he and the other staff always immediately covered their nose and mouth with surgical masks.

Nami asked what time the man with the silver spectacles would come in to work.

The chief librarian looked puzzled. 'The man with the silver spectacles?'

'Yes. A tall young man.'

'I'm the only male staff member in this library,' he replied. 'Several of the staff do wear glasses, but all of them are women.'

'He comes and tells me when the library's about to close.'

'Hmm.'

'That sounds like Takuya,' a member of the support staff, busy at her computer, piped up, looking over her shoulder.

'Ah, yes. Of course.' The chief librarian nodded and smiled.

'Takuya?'

'Well, Takuya's not one of our official team. I don't know how to describe him, really. One of our regulars. He should be here. But he's not . . . That's strange.'

'Today's the day he goes in to hospital. He goes in Wednesday mornings.'

'Ah yes. Well then, he'll be in this afternoon.'

'His mother will be with him.'

After a nap in a corner of the children's reading nook, Nami woke up to find Takuya there. He was sitting in a window seat absorbed in a compendium on tropical fish. His mother did not seem to be about. Nami edged closer, but he looked so engrossed she did not want to disturb him. When he let her out at the door, she gave him a brief nod and ran straight back to the square.

She sat down on the bench. She had absolutely nothing with her. Nothing to eat, drink, no change of clothes, not even a blanket. All she had were her thoughts. Apparently that was all she would need.

And still Nanao didn't come. Night came, and then morning, then another night and another morning. Yet another night came and yet another morning. On and on, in an endless succession of nights and mornings, but still no one. Until one day, who knows how much time later, having waited and waited, Nami visited a public toilet in the park, and caught sight of her own face in the mirror. She cried out in shock.

Who was that?! The person in the mirror was like a mountain witch. Withered grimy skin, dull sunken eyes, hollow cheeks, dry stiff hair falling over her shoulders and breasts, a stooped back, head thrust forward . . .

How would Nanao recognise her looking like this? He might have come to the park any number of times and walked straight by.

Quickly, Nami found an elastic band on the floor and bound her hair; she washed her face, and rubbed her cheeks to bring some colour back into her skin. She straightened up her spine, and squeezed and raised her shoulder blades. That was a bit better, perhaps.

And she also, just to make sure, moved to a different bench – one easily spotted by passers-by.

She raised her chin, and sat up straight.

But she ought maybe to have some back-up prop . . . some object about her, in her hands, simple and obvious, that would help him make the connection. Something that he would immediately associate with his mother, that would provide unquestionable proof.

In a flash, an idea came. Animal crackers! They had been a staple of Nanao's diet, and hers, in those early days together. Boxes and boxes of them had come from the doctor. What better piece of personal data could there be! Something only he and she knew. If she held an animal cracker in her hand it would take him back to their past, no matter how raggedy and unclean she looked. Maybe he would share a cracker with her, in celebration of having found her . . . But how to get hold of such crackers . . . She would have to steal some, from a convenience store or a supermarket. But what if while she was busy doing that, Nanao passed by her bench? Then she would miss him.

Takuya had told her she should make sure to

keep an eye out. His words now weighed heavily on her. They were like a curse.

What should she do? Go to the shop? Or stay here?

Just then, something landed with a light crash in front of her. A dark pink cardboard box. She could hardly believe her eyes. The box was decorated with cute little cartoons of animals.

Animal crackers! What? How come?

Instinctively, she got up. Before her stood a man in a flat cap.

With surly glances, the man tossed another box over. This one was a box of chocolate cookies. The boxes were coming from a big crate by his feet. Next was a box of savoury snacks. And now a box of plain cookies.

Right in front of her, there was a display table. When had that been set up? The pile of novelty goods on it only grew. *Bang, bang, smash, thud, crunch.* Cookies, dolls, games, alarm clocks, cuddly toys, and lucky cat figurines in shiny gold, beckoning . . . What on earth was this . . . ? In a few minutes, every inch of the table top was covered.

'Move! Get off the bench.' Two youths in tee shirts were waiting to remove her bench. As she got up and followed them, she noticed a little mini truck whizz by. Come to think of it, there seemed to be mini trucks and vans all over the square. They carried her bench to join a stack of others deposited behind the public toilets, where there were a lot of scraggy uncut bushes. As she watched, people strode back and forth carrying steel poles and rails and pieces of red cloth and white cloth. There were shouts and the noise of things being hammered together. People were building round carnival booths. Some were red, and some were white. Some had tin roofs, some had blue tarpaulins. Banners went up, and strings of lights were hung at the entrances. In just a few minutes, the square was transformed into a venue for a festival.

A leaflet was blowing around at Nami's feet. *Satsuki Town's Fun-Filled Funfair. In Satsuki Town's*

Park No. 1. Friday October 29 – Saturday October 30 – Sunday October 31.

The place Nami had been sitting had been the last space left to fill. The man in the flat cap lifted wooden stands of various sizes out from the back of his van, and set them where the bench had been. He arrayed his products. They were cookies, toys and ornaments – prizes for a game.

The man in the flat cap gave her a sideways glance. She pretended to be transfixed by a plastic bag filled with a huge number of goldfish. He tipped them all straight into a blue tank, and the next minute they were all swimming nonchalantly in the water.

The funfair was going to last three days. How could she get her hands on those animal crackers?

The man glanced at her again. Suspiciously, as if he'd read her mind.

As dusk fell, people came to the fair. Couples pressed closely together, children thrilled to bits. Girls in yukata despite the chill in the air, pointing at things in the open-air stalls and shrieking in merry excitement. A melody blared out along with a crackling sound from a radio-cassette player, playing a song all about the town. Everywhere the voices of old friends greeting each other loudly. 'Hi! How have you been? Haven't seen you for ages! Are you well?'

A crowd gathered in front of the man's booth. He had exchanged his flat cap for a towel twisted into a headband, worn jauntily on his bald pate. Standing at his table, 'Line up! Line up!' he shouted. And he clapped his hands briskly.

Nami edged closer towards the animal crackers, extremely slowly so he wouldn't notice. One step, then two steps . . . pretending to be looking at the other booths. Finally, she was right by the toys and ornaments. The man did not try to shoo her away. But the moment she put out her hand, he turned on her, threateningly, with a furious expression on his face. Try anything, and he would catch her in the act. Nami waited for her moment. Any number of times, she was on the point of stretching out and taking a box. When he was packing carrier bags with novelty goods, when he was chatting with customers, when he was checking that he had enough change . . . But Day One ended with no crackers in hand.

Once the fair-goers had left, the traders quietly tidied up, and leaving their carnival booths up they loaded their wares into their trucks. The man took off his headband, and took his flat cap from his pocket. He glanced at her, then got into his van, and drove off without a word.

Day Two. The weather was dull and overcast. At four, the mini trucks and vans began to arrive. The man arranged the prizes in the same place as before, looking suspiciously over at her as he unpacked. The animal crackers came out last. With exaggerated care he placed them gently on top of the table. He turned the box so that it would face her.

Splot. A raindrop fell right on the perky lion's nose.

At about five, the rain started pouring down. The man stood up from his collapsible chair, balled up the newspaper he'd been using to shield his head, and hurled it to the ground. He whipped the plastic covering from his goods, and packed them all back in the cardboard box. He pushed Nami out of his way, and carried everything off to his parked van. 'You packing up?' asked a fellow trader who sold squid on sticks. But he got no reply. The other traders prepared to sit it out at the back of their booths, relaxing and smoking cigarettes and listening to the radio.

The man got into his van, slamming the door. Winding down the window, he yelled over to Nami. 'Hey.' He indicated the back seat with the thumb of his hand. Was he telling her to get in? Nami shook her head. In the end he simply snorted, and drove off.

Day Three. The rain let up at first light. Nami had spent the whole night alone, as the other traders eventually left too. At one point in the night, a mother and her daughter had come along, under a red umbrella. 'See? The funfair's not open today,' the mother told her child in a loving, tender tone. The child had carried on sobbing in her red raincoat. And then they'd disappeared. The sound of the sobbing child lingered in Nami's ears.

And now, once again, she was standing right next to the boxes of animal crackers. Just a few centimetres away. The man wasn't looking her way. It was the last day, and a long queue had formed in front of the man's booth.

Maybe he was intending to pounce on her as soon as she tried to take one. Or maybe he was trying to tell her, *please go ahead.*

It didn't matter either way. Nami wouldn't have been able to take one even if she'd tried. Since about midnight, her body seemed to have shut down. It was strange. The voice of the man shouting for people to line up line up was like the roar of an animal in distant mountains. The festival's recorded music, the laughter of all sorts of unknown people, the sizzling sound of grilled squid from the nearby stall, and a regular *pop* or a *bang*: everything was coming from far away.

She was drifting in and out of consciousness. *I have to stay awake,* she told herself. But try as she might, it already seemed hopeless. The contours of the boxes of animal biscuits were starting to blur. Everything seemed to be covered in a light red mist.

And then she thought she heard a voice: 'Mum?' Her closing eyelids fluttered open.

'Mum?' Was she hearing things?

'Mum. Is that you?'

It wasn't her imagination. It was Nanao's voice.

She couldn't believe it. Nanao was standing right in front of her! Silently, she called to him again and again.

'Mum!'

Nanao had grown up – he was an adult. He had been only seven when they'd had to part. How old was he now? He wore a blue long-sleeved shirt. And jeans. He had a watch on his wrist. Nanao! He really was there!

The instant Nanao reached out and tried to touch her, the man with the twisted towel on his head bawled:

'SCRAM!'

Nanao withdrew his hand.

'Do not touch. And no skipping the queue. Line up! Line up!' The man jostled Nanao to the end of the line.

Just behind Nanao, Nami could see a young woman in a dress. The young woman was staring at her.

'Hey,' the young woman said. 'Is that someone you know?'

'That's my mother.'

'Your mother?'

'Yep. My biological mother. I told you about her, right? I was taken away from her when I was a child.'

' . . . Oh. You don't say . . .'

The young woman looked over at Nami as if trying to see what she might be worth.

'Well, what's she doing there?'

'She's been waiting for me.'

At this, Nami knew that the waves of her thoughts had reached the shore.

The woman seemed to be Nanao's sweetheart.

She pulled on his arm, and clasped his hand in hers. She put on a babyish voice. 'You know what?' she said. 'I'm hungry. I wanna eat.'

'In a minute, okay?'

'No.' The young woman stamped her foot. 'I hate this place. I want some takoyaki!'

'Can you not go and eat without me?'

'Whaa . . . ? I wanna do it with you! I'll get fat otherwise!'

'Just leave half for me. I'll be over right away.'

'Really? You mean that?'

'I promise.'

'Okay, meet you in front of the tent. Be there, okay?'

Nanao watched her leave, then directed his attention to Nami. About ten people were standing in the queue.

Nanao shouted, enunciating his words clearly: 'Mum, don't go yet. It won't be long. My turn's coming up.'

Nami nodded happily. Tears were coursing down her cheeks. What a kind, thoughtful boy!

The line slowly got shorter. With every step, Nanao sent Nami a nod. *It won't be long now.*

Ahead of Nanao was a young father, holding the hand of a little girl.

'Dad. Look. Animal crackers. I want those!'

'Don't you worry.'

'It's 100 yen.' The vendor held out a hand.

The father gave him a coin. The man tossed it into a basket, and handed the father a plastic rifle.

'Papa, do your best!'

The father brimmed with confidence. 'Watch me.'

The father put the rifle up against his chest. He took aim at the animal crackers . . . and with a one, two, three, he pulled the trigger and fired.

Pop. A cork pellet shot out, and – of course – hit the target.

'Dad!'

'Amazing, aren't I?'

Father and daughter excitedly took their prize. The man set about preparing for the next person to take a shot, putting out a fresh box. He pulled back the rifle's lever, and took a fresh cork out of his pocket.

Nanao handed him his 100-yen coin. The man handed him the rifle and stepped back.

Nanao took no time at all. Without bothering to steady the gun against his chest, he pointed it straight at Nami, and fired.

The cork pellet hit Nami on her shoulder. *Plock.*

Nami was sent reeling. Her feet stayed on the ground, but her upper body tilted sideways, and then, as if a thread had been drawn out of her, she crumpled and fell straight down to the ground.

Thunk. The back of her ear caught a corner of the stall. As she lay there, face up, a second later there was another sound: *donk.* A heavy fortune-beckoning cat, which constituted the 'Grand Prize', had landed on her face.

'A direct hit! Right between the eyes!' The man banged a gong.

Nanao set down the rifle. Seeing him leave, the man shouted:

'Hey! What about your prize!'

'I don't want her.'

'Hey now. That's not right. You gotta play by the rules. Otherwise . . .'

'I told you, I don't want her.'

'Hey. Are you going to take it – or not?' The man grabbed Nanao by the shoulder.

Just then they heard someone calling. 'Nanao, are you coming?! Your takoyaki's getting cold!'

Nanao knocked the man's hand away, and rushed off.

'Humph!' The man scratched his bald head. Then, straightening himself up, he called out to passers-by: 'He-e-y, is someone going to do me a favour and take that guy's prize? No money needed!'

No takers came forward. One or two people did approach, curious, wanting to see what was being offered, but as soon as they saw Nami lying there with blood pouring from the top and sides of her head, they let out a shriek and skedaddled.

One person, though, did seem to be hanging around. He peered down anxiously at Nami. He was wearing spectacles.

'Takuya,' she muttered.

'Are you all right?'

'Un-huh.'

She smiled at him.

Was that his mother there, just behind? Such a loving mother . . . Takuya gave a little nod, and then he and his mother vanished into thin air.

In a complete change from the hustle and bustle of a few seconds before, the stall was now hushed. No customers approached. They didn't want to be near her.

'Goddamn it!' the bald man swore, dropping his head in his hands. He glanced disgustedly at Nami, who lay there, still bleeding profusely, on the ground. He gave an enormous sigh, then, looking annoyed at having to do it, leaned down, grasped her by the ankles and lifted her legs. He dragged her to the bushes behind the public toilets, taking her beyond the stacked-up benches, much further, and tipped her into the place where there was a lot of scraggy uncut undergrowth. He picked some weeds, covered her belly with them as best he could, then took a piss in the public toilet, and went off.

In a little while his voice could be heard, shouting his usual patter. *Line up line up. Fun for all the family.*

Nami listened, gazing up at the night sky. It was inky black. As well as the man's voice, she could hear all sorts of other sounds coming from the fair. The squeaky sounds that thin plastic bags made as they were put over blobs of candy floss, the crisp sound of cellophane coverings being torn off toffee apples, the sharp snap of wooden disposable chopsticks being broken apart, the sound of the goldfish making leaps above the surface of the water, the sound of bubbles, the sound of her own heart.

Nami did not die for the longest time.

A few hours later, the funfair came to an end, and the only sounds were the sounds of insects. But she had not died.

She wondered indifferently when the end might come.

She could see no moon in the sky, and no stars either.

A few drops of rain fell during the night.

The light in the morning was white and very faint.

Up in the sky, everyone who had died before her was waiting impatiently for her to make an appearance. 'Come on, Nami. Hurry up . . .'

When she did finally arrive, they all ran up to her, and gathered around.

'It's over. Finally!'

'You did well. You didn't give up.'

And then they all held her in the tightest embrace.

A NIGHT
TO REMEMBER

For fifteen years after leaving school I was unemployed. How did I spend my time? Lazing around at home, sprawled on the tatami, watching TV, and eating snacks. Every day I was shouted at by my father. 'Go out and get yourself a job,' he would say, 'and if you won't do that, leave – get out, now.' I didn't feel like doing either. I just wanted to carry on the way I was – lying idly around. Until the day I died.

I'd been a bit unwilling to bestir myself since childhood. If I'd had my way, I wouldn't have gone to school at all, and would have stayed at home, doing nothing. But my father wasn't having it. So at least until the end of middle school I made a special effort and left the house, to complete as much schooling as I had to, legally. I didn't have great memories of the world out there.

As time passed spending whole days doing very

little, I gradually started to feel that being bipedal was simply not worth the trouble, and I decided I would try as much as possible not to stand up at all. If I had to get around I would do it by dragging myself forward by my elbows, on my belly.

So there I lay, all day and every day – basically prone. It didn't make any difference whether I was awake or fast asleep. Occasionally, I would drag myself out of the room across the hall to go to the toilet. I arranged everything I needed – the TV, packs of tissues, the remote control, manga – so it was lying within my reach. When I got hungry, I simply grabbed one of the small packets of cookies scattered about on the floor, and if I didn't see any cookies, there was always the cat's food. While I was about it, I sometimes even used my cat's litter tray. The cat and I had some big fights about this.

One day I was doing my usual thing of lying on the floor watching TV, and my dad started giving me one of his sermons. Oh not again, I thought, and I ignored him. The sermon went on and on – and on. Halfway through I had an urge to go to the toilet, so I dragged myself out of the room and used the litter tray. When I got back, my father was waiting with a rolled-up news-paper, and he now started whacking me on the head, over and over. I darted this way and that, to keep out of his reach. At least on the tatami, I was the nimblest. My dad was now quite old, and his hips were bothering him, even though as a young man he'd enjoyed going on hikes up Mount Fuji, so every time he lunged to grab me, he would cry out, 'Ouch! Ooh, ooh, the pain!' I shot straight through his legs, and out into the corridor. 'Get out! Just leave!' I heard him yell behind me. So I just carried on – into the hallway, and out through the unlocked front door.

It had been a rushed exit, but the air outside, which I hadn't smelled in a long time, was really quite pleasant. I could feel the heat of the day caught in the asphalt rising up through my palms, and the rays of the sun gently setting aglow the whole of my back. It was late May, as I recall. I kept going, racing onward, dragging myself forward along the road. I didn't have any idea of where I was heading. Pretty soon my father's mood would simmer down, I calculated. I forged ahead, moving over to the side of the road to take a nap whenever exhaustion got the better of me, and then, when I'd recovered, pressing on.

After about my fourth nap, I realised I had completely lost my bearings. It felt like I had travelled a considerable distance, but where on earth had I started from? I was definitely hearing more footsteps around me, compared to when I had set out. My low line of sight made it impossible for me to get any idea of what my surroundings looked like, but I got the distinct impression that I was nearing a place with crowds of people, like a railway station or a shopping street. By now, dusk was approaching, and my stomach was grumbling.

Directly in front of me I saw some popcorn, so I picked up a piece and popped it in my mouth. Mm. Nice and salty. The cat food had given me a taste for savoury things. Glancing about, I saw puffs of popcorn scattered about in quite a few

places. First eating one piece, then another, I fran-
tically followed the trail. Luckily, passers-by simply
let me get on with it. I'd been out of the house for
a few hours now, and so far most of the legs had
given me a wide berth, or simply stepped over me.
Maybe the world wasn't such a scary place after
all. Only once did someone tread right down on
my back. They gave me a stammering and profuse
apology. 'S-s-sorry! I didn't see you there!' I felt
quite guilty. I was the one who should apologise,
lying stretched out there at the edge of the road.

I'd come to the end of the trail of popcorn. I
looked about for any other scraps.

All of a sudden it started to rain. I wandered
about a little, uncertain, looking for a suitable
shelter. While I was doing this the rain got hard-
er, pelting down around me. By the time I finally
found a place where the ground was dry, night had
fallen.

I now found myself at one end of a covered
shopping arcade. It seemed well past closing time.
On either side, rows of closed grey shutters were

pulled down to the ground, and in front of them cardboard boxes and bin bags had been put out for collection.

That popcorn hadn't had any staying power. My stomach felt like a hollow pit. I crept forward, looking all about for any scraps of food lying on the ground, and my attention was caught by one small black plastic bin bag that had been placed all by itself in front of one of the shops. As I approached, a deliciously fragrant, greasy smell met my nostrils. I undid the knot at the top, and peeped inside. The bag was full of croquettes, broken up into chunks.

With the end of my finger, I hooked out a piece, and took a bite. The delicate taste of mashed potato – sweet but not too sweet – swept over my taste buds. The slightly grainy texture of the ground meat and onion, the fluffy creaminess of the potato, the crisp texture of the fried bread-crumb mixture encasing both, all of it drenched in oil, dispelled my sense of tiredness. I attacked the croquettes, filling my mouth, not caring how I might look. Once I'd got through them, a resounding burp escaped me.

But at that moment, I got a strong sense that I wasn't alone.

Something was directly behind me. I was sure of it. Was it . . . a cat? No, it was definitely an animal of some size. Maybe a dog. Or an inoshishi. I couldn't work it out, but I got the distinct impression of its eyes boring into the back of my head. Slowly, very cautiously, I twisted my head round to take a look. I got the shock of my life. My heart almost stopped. It was a human!

A human male. With long hair. Nearly half of his face was covered with a beard and whiskers. I was astounded to see that he was flat out on the ground, just like me.

Lying there on his belly, he was observing me steadily. For a while, we simply stared at each other, absolutely still, as if held down by some force, unable to unlock our gaze.

He was the one who moved first. Slowly, using his elbows, he dragged himself forward across the road that separated us. I for my part slowly brought my body around, one bit at a time, so I could face him head-on.

He made a few moves forward, then a few more, and I did the same, matching him. The gap between us shrank quickly. Two metres. One metre. Ten centimetres. Five centimetres. One centimetre. Now, the soft, furry part of his face was all but touching the tip of my nose . . . But then a blinding beam of light lit up both of our faces.

'Look out!' the man screamed. The groaning sounds of an engine, like the roaring of the earth, bore down on us. I found myself grabbed by the arm, and as fast as we could we scurried to the side of the road.

It was a truck. We waited for the sound of the tyres to disappear into the distance.

Finally the man spoke.

'That was the rubbish truck. Every night around this time they come.'

'Goodness me . . .'

My heart was beating very fast.

'In a few minutes it'll do a U-turn and come back. Let's get out of here.'

The man turned round, and headed towards a little alley between two shops in the arcade, down which he disappeared. I quickly followed him.

Seemingly familiar with the path, the man shunted himself smoothly forward in the darkness. I, in contrast, bumped my head against hard objects, and got my legs tangled up in what I could only assume were plastic carrier bags. It took some time for me to get anywhere at all. When I finally emerged at the other end, there he was, waiting. 'Are you all right?' he asked, when I caught up with him. I nodded.

'Yeah. Just about.'

'From here on, it's safe. This road is Pedestrians and Bicycles Only.'

We now dragged ourselves forward side by side. The rain had, rather abruptly, stopped. I asked the man where we were headed. 'We're going to my house,' he said.

In barely any time at all, he came to a halt. We

were in front of something like a frame of metal bars.

'Here we are.' It was the gate to his house. The man pushed the gate open with his forehead and went on in. The gate gave a high-pitched squeak.

Beyond the gate was a door. The man tapped at the door. *Rat-a-tat-tat*. A special knock. A light flicked on in the hall. After a moment, the door was opened quietly. Over the man's shoulders, I caught a glimpse of two ankles in white socks.

'This is my mum,' the man told me.

A little perplexed at this turn of events, I half wondered whether I should turn and head back, but I wished her a good evening, nevertheless.

His mum was carrying a towel. Her face was out of view, but she was wearing an apron that was white, matching her socks. Quickly she gave the man's soaking-wet beard and whiskers a brisk rub-down. Her hands were plump and white, and on the third finger of her left hand was a silver ring. Once that was done, she towel-dried my hair as well, hard, with the same towel. Feeling a bit disconcerted, I nevertheless voiced my thanks, a little apologetically.

'Thank you.'

His mum still hadn't said a word.

The man pulled himself inside, into the hall, which was on the same level as the entranceway, and then headed down the corridor. 'Come on,' he said, with a look back over his shoulder.

His mum took up a position ahead of him to lead the way. Her pink slippers flapped slowly and softly along the floor. He followed her, and I followed him. On the smooth polished flooring my arms and legs slid about as I pulled myself along. With each move forward, my nails made a scrabbling sound, and the man glanced back, amused. At the end of the corridor we emerged into a big open space.

'This is the living room,' the man said. We progressed over a carpet with a complicated pattern. Once we were over the carpet, we headed down yet another corridor.

'This is a storage room.' 'This is the toilet.' The door to the storage room was a sliding one. From the crack under the door to the toilet I detected the fragrance of an air freshener. This house was an enormous mansion. 'I don't know what's here behind this door,' the man told me. 'This one too. I have no idea.' We passed by any number of doors.

At some point, his mum's white socks and pink slippers vanished from view. At the end of the corridor the man took a turn to the left, and then stopped in front of a fusuma. The paper was ripped to pieces.

'This is my room.' Putting a finger into one of the rips in the paper, he slid the fusuma to one side.

'Come on in,' he said.

It was a room with tatami mats.

'Make yourself comfortable. My mum'll bring us some refreshments in a second.'

Duly, I went inside. The room was drab, with no ornaments. A TV, an alarm clock, a remote control, a pillow and packs of tissues, all placed on the tatami. A couple of low bookcases, two shelves only, lined with nothing but pocket-sized books. That was all. In front of one bookcase were three zabuton stowed one on top of the other, and next to them a pile of towels. In one corner lay several sheets of newspaper, and beneath them I caught a glimpse of a cat litter tray.

Directly in front of me was a long tube hanging down in a big loop from somewhere I couldn't see. It puzzled me. I craned my neck to get a view. Where did it come from? It was attached to something that looked like a huge glass globe.

'That's my water.'

The man stretched out, grabbed hold of the tube, put it to his mouth, and took a gulp. 'My mum replenishes my drinking water every day.'

All of a sudden, the fusuma slid open silently and something was pushed into the room.

'Thanks!' the man said. The fusuma slid shut.

It was a tray. The man stretched out and drew it closer. On the tray were two beakers with straws, two moist towels and two cupcakes. After using the moist towel to wipe his hands, the man took one of the cakes, and motioned for me to do the same.

'Eat up. These are good.'

I could see sliced almonds on top of a perfectly baked light-brown pastry crust.

'Thank you, I will!' Forgetting all about the croquettes I'd stuffed down earlier, I finished it off in no time at all.

'I enjoyed that!'

'You made quick work of it, didn't you!' The man smiled.

'Why wouldn't I? I've never eaten anything so delicious!'

'I know. My mum makes these cakes.'

'They're home-made? Wow!'

'My mum is a cake-baking genius.' He looked very pleased with himself. 'Japanese confections, western cakes and desserts . . . you name it, whatever she bakes, it's great. And not only cakes. Her everyday cooking is out-of-this-world good.'

It seemed like he was pretty proud of his mum. And yet, she still hadn't said a word to me.

'Do you think your mum feels okay about me? I get the feeling she thinks I'm a nuisance?'

'No. Why'd you say that?'

'Well, I did just turn up unannounced . . . And just now, when I said good evening, she didn't say a word back.'

'Oh, that's just her way.' The man laughed. 'Don't worry, it's fine. She never talks to me, either. It's always me who talks to her. It's like a one-way thing.'

'So you don't *talk*? Not even with your own *mother*?'

'Nuh-uh. Mind you, that's not because we don't get on. She's a really nice person. She's the one who sees to all my needs. She brings me things to eat, she replenishes the water in my water dispenser, she changes my litter, she adjusts the air conditioning . . . She cleans my room, and she does my laundry. And every Saturday she gives me a bath. Oh. What day is today, by the way?'

'She must love you, terribly.'

'Well . . . I don't know about that. It's just that she's a very caring person.'

The man grabbed the remote, and switched on

the TV. 'Oh, it's the *Wasshoi!* quiz. That must mean it's Thursday.'

The man pulled over two zabuton, pushed one in my direction, and used the other to rest his chin on. Keeping his eyes fixed on the TV screen, when the quiz master began posing questions, he yelled out the answers, quicker than anyone in the show.

'Uesugi Kenshin!'

'. . . Correct! Wow, you really know a lot!'

'Of course. History is my best subject.'

So it seemed. Looking at the many paperbacks lining the bookshelves, I realised that they were all historical novels.

'Yamaguchi Prefecture!'

'. . . Correct again! I'm impressed!'

For a while, the man became completely wrapped up in answering the quiz. When the ad break came on, I finally asked what his name was.

'The name's Jack,' he told me. That's strange, I thought. To me he had an unmistakably Asian face.

'Don't laugh,' he added.

'I'm not,' I said. 'Did your mum give you that name?'

'No. Her little boy did.' And then Jack continued: 'Noboru. He's at primary school. Third year, possibly? I imagine he's taking his bath right now.'

'So he's your little brother?'

'He and I don't really see eye to eye.' Jack scowled. 'He used to be sweet. But recently, he's got quite violent in the way he talks and behaves. Frankly, he gets me down. He's always bossing me about, as if I should pay any attention to him.'

'So your *little brother* gave you your name?'

'I told you, he and I aren't brothers – not really. Noboru was the person who found me. At that time, he was in kindergarten. Jack was the name of the main character in an anime he happened to be crazy about at the time. I don't mind the name really, but I would have preferred it if my mum had been the one to give my name to me. Not him.'

'Wait. You mean your mum isn't your real mum?'

'No, no. She is.'

Just then, we heard footsteps. *Slap slap slap.* Feet that had no slippers or socks.

'Here he comes . . .' said Jack.

The fusuma slid open violently, and we heard a loud voice fill the room.

'WOW! I CAN'T BELIEVE IT! UWAA!'

Two skinny legs, burnt brown by the sun, stomped towards us across the tatami, and a similarly sunburnt face swooped down and peered up at me from below.

'So you actually found one!'

'This is Noboru,' Jack said under his breath.

'Mum! Mum!' Noboru yelled, turning his face to the corridor.

'Y-e-e-su!' we heard, from somewhere far away.

'Get in here! Quickly!'

In a moment, there were the feet with white socks just beyond the fusuma.

'Look!' Noboru pointed a finger at my face.

'I know,' his mum replied. She had a much lower voice than I expected.

'What . . . ? You know? Why? How?'

'Well, who else but I would have brought them the refreshments?'

'No way! Why didn't you tell me first?'

'How could I? You were having your bath.'

'But why didn't you tell me as soon as you could? I would have liked to be the one to give them cake! It's always you, Mum! That's so mean of you!'

'Oh? So will that mean that from tomorrow, you'll be the one who brings them their cakes? You'll bring them their drinks, see to their water, and put out their food? You'll lay out their mattresses, and change their litter, and give them their bath?'

'Sure I will!'

'Nothing but fibs. What about when you picked Jack up and brought him home? You said you were going to look after him all by yourself. But who really had to do it, in the end? It ended up being Mum who did everything, didn't it?'

'This time, I'm really going to do it! I'll do everything, starting tomorrow! Mum, you mustn't do anything!'

'Right, sure . . .'

'Wow, amazing! So he's managed to actually find one – and bring her back! Who knew?! Jack's quite the popular guy!'

His mum gave a chuckle. 'So it seems.'

'Wonder whether they're going to have a baby?!'

'Not right away. That's too much.'

'Well then, when? When do you think?'

'She's only just got here. Maybe she'll have a baby when she's settled in.'

'Well, I want them to have a baby soon. I've been thinking of babies' names anyway. Here's what I've come up with. It's going to be either King, or Toad, or Gorimaru. One of those three. I wonder which name'll be best . . . ?'

'But those are all boys' names. What happens if she has a girl baby?'

'I can't do girls' names – they're difficult. Mum, you've got to think of one.'

'Well . . . let's see. How about Happy-chan?'

'Ugh! That doesn't sound right.'

'Really? I think it's rather nice. Well, what about calling this one Happy-chan?'

'Okay! I'll allow it . . . Hey, you! You're going to be called Happy-chan! Is that okay by you?'

I dipped my head, feeling utterly confused.

The boy laughed triumphantly. 'She agreed! Seems like she likes it! Hey, Happy-chan! You and Jack are going to get married tonight, okay? And you're going to have lots of kids!'

'Well, how about waiting till tomorrow for the next instalment? It's time for bed now.'

'I don't want to go to bed! I want to wait up till Dad comes home!'

'Dad's going to be late tonight. I told you, don't you remember? He has a meeting. It'll be midnight by the time he returns.'

'Well then, I'm going to wait up till midnight!'

'Hey! Stop messing about!'

Thwap! He got a swift rap on the head.

'Okay, I got the point! Right, wait there. Back in one second.'

Noboru dashed out of the room. In a flash he was back.

'This is for you,' he said. He put a little carton of

milk in front of me. 'And one for you, Jack.'

'Thanks,' Jack said.

His mum opened the closet, and dragged out mattresses. While she and Noboru were arranging our bedding, Jack and I withdrew to a far corner of the room. There was a pair of mattresses, with two pillows, one for each of us.

'Goodnight, Jack and Happy-chan!'

'Goodnight,' Jack replied.

The fusuma was pulled shut, and their footsteps disappeared down the corridor. Now, once again, we were alone together. The quiz programme on TV seemed to have come to an end; now it was the news, with images of a meteorite that someone in some country or other had apparently seen falling out of the sky.

I had quite a few questions that I wanted to put to Jack. I was wondering where I should start, but before I'd even said a word he broke the silence.

'So, I guess that means you're Happy-chan!'

'Don't laugh,' I retorted.

'I'm not,' was the reply. 'I think it's cute. Trust

my mum – she's got such good taste. Compare that to the names Noboru came up with. What did he say? King? Toad? Gorimaru? With those names you'd have to be kind of like . . . strong and hefty.'

'Noboru did mention something about names for babies.'

'Uh-huh.'

'What was that all about? Am I going to be having your babies?'

'Oh, well, um . . . That is . . .'

'Noboru did say that, didn't he? He said you'd "found me and brought me back".'

'Uh-huh.'

'What did he mean by that?'

'Ermmmm.' Jack scratched his beard, looking nervous. 'Well, if I'm honest, Noboru's been on at me for a while now. Telling me I should go out and get myself a wife.'

'A wife.'

'The guy's fixated. He just keeps on and on, never gives up – till I do as he says. So recently, I've been out on the prowl every night, looking for a bride. But it's been hard, and I haven't found anybody. Tonight, finally, well . . . I did. Of course, if you don't want to, that's totally fine . . . You can say no. It's okay.'

Jack was looking down at the floor, embarrassed.

I realised I was being proposed to, by the very first person I'd met since I'd left home.

'So . . . you want . . . me? You think I'm good enough?'

'Of course!'

Jack's breath came up against my face. I caught a whiff of the cake that he'd eaten earlier. Jack looked straight into my eyes, and said:

'I want you, and you only.'

You, and you only. My feelings exactly. The instant our eyes met, back in that alley, I had known. That he had to be my special someone. I gave a quick nod to express my gratitude.

'Well then, yes, if you'll have me.'

'She said yes! Phew!' Jack breathed a big sigh of relief. Then, reaching for the carton of milk that Noboru had left us, he carefully removed the transparent plastic sleeve for the drinking straw, and wrapped it around the ring finger of my left hand, tying it tightly.

'This can do as your ring.'

The two of us lay on the futon mattresses that his mum had laid out for us, and drank our milk. As we drank, we pushed up against each other with our foreheads, chuckling quietly as we did so. Jack's beard felt so ticklingly soft as over and over again he pressed it up against my nose and along my cheeks that I could barely keep the milk from spilling out of my mouth. When I ran away from home in the morning, who would have dreamed this would occur? Would this be the start of countless days spent lying around with Jack, drinking milk? And maybe there would be a King, and a Toad, and a Gorimaru chuckling and chortling and drinking their milk along with us.

I still couldn't believe that it was happening. But happening it was. The plastic sleeve serving as my ring twinkled on my finger.

With a start, I remembered my father. How

would he react when I told him I was going to get married? I had never had anyone to call even an acquaintance, still less a boyfriend. My father was going to be astounded, I was sure. Maybe he would even shed tears of joy. I knew I had been nothing but a burden to him, but finally I was going to be able to make him stop worrying about me and feel reassured about my future.

I glanced at the alarm clock. It was very nearly ten. Almost twelve hours since I'd been thrown out of the house. That had to be long enough, surely, for my father to have cooled down.

'Hey, Jack. What about coming back home with me? Right now?'

Jack, the straw in his mouth, threw me a look of horror.

'Back . . . home?'

'To my house. To my family.'

'You mean . . . you actually have a house?'

'Yes. Well, it's not my house. It belongs to my father.'

'Your father? So you have a father?'

'Yes! Though I don't have a mother. I just want to introduce you, and tell my father all about you. I know it's kind of late, but I should be getting home now anyway. My father will be getting anxious. I just thought it might be nice, in view of what's happened, if you were to come too . . .'

'What are you talking about? You must be mad. No way.'

'What do you mean?'

'What do I mean? Well . . . I can't do that!'

'Well, surely you can come and introduce yourself, and tell him formally. "Hi there, Dad, we're going to get married!" That's all it would require.'

'You say that like it's that simple. Introduce myself? You've got to know that's not on.'

Jack looked sad for a moment.

'So there's no way you'll do it?'

'No. Sorry.'

'Okay. That's a pity but . . . I'll just have to go by myself, then. I'll be back tomorrow morning.' I dragged myself over the futon, and reached up to a rip in the fusuma to pull it open.

'No! You mustn't go!' Jack grabbed hold of one of my ankles, quite roughly, and hauled me back.

'Hey! Do you mind?! All I plan to do is go and tell my father what's happened. I'm coming back. I'll be back tomorrow morning.'

'I don't want you to leave me.'

'But I don't have a choice . . . Okay, well, how about if I come back before dawn.'

'You mean that?'

'I mean it.'

'You will come back? You really mean it?'

'I will.'

'I have this sneaking feeling you're going to leave me forever.'

'I'm going to come back.'

'Do you promise?'

'I promise.'

Jack gently released my ankle.

We linked our little fingers together and made a pinky promise.

As I emerged into the corridor, somewhere I heard the sound of someone taking a shower.

Probably his mum. Noboru was surely tucked up peacefully in bed. There was no shouting or stomping to be heard.

I set out towards the hallway, but 'Not that way,' said Jack, who had followed me out. 'At this time of night the front door will be locked. It's this door here.' He pointed to the sliding door he'd described on our way in as the storeroom.

I pushed it open to find a pitch-black space. I went straight in, and immediately banged my head against something hard – it felt like a box. 'Easy does it,' Jack said. Squeezing ourselves past furniture legs and up through the narrow gaps between cardboard boxes we managed somehow or other to get over to a window.

'There's a way out here. The lock's broken.' Jack pulled back the bottom of the curtain.

'Thanks.'

I opened the window just wide enough for me to slip out. A cold wind hit me in the face. It was much brighter outside, because of the streetlights.

There was a bit of a drop, so I lowered myself

down, carefully placing my hands firmly on the grass. I glanced back to see Jack's face. He was gazing at me, with a look as if he might burst into tears at any moment. That was when I realised something. Underneath the beard that covered his face, Jack was really still just a kid.

'Will you explain to your mum . . . ?'

'I'll tell her,' Jack said.

'I'll be right back.'

'I'll be waiting.'

Once past the wall, I headed right, as Jack had directed me to, which brought me to the front gate. I gave it a nudge with my forehead, but it didn't open, so I crawled under it and out onto the street.

It was only once I'd got to the other end of the narrow alleyway and emerged into the shopping arcade that I realised I'd committed the stupidest blunder. Which way should I head now? I had no idea, because I hadn't the faintest idea of which direction my house lay in.

How thoughtless of me. And come to think of it, where was I anyway? I didn't even know the name of the neighbourhood. I should go back and ask Jack for a map. I had just turned around when suddenly everything in front of my eyes turned dazzling bright, and for the second time that day I heard that horrendous sound like the roaring of the earth, the sound of an engine, right by my ears . . . I had no time to make a dash for it. I didn't stand a chance. I was run right over.

I had been hit by the rubbish truck. An employee of the municipal government was at the wheel, so an article about it appeared in the newspapers. 'It's not something you expect,' the man apparently told the police. 'A person sleeping right in the middle of the road . . .' I picked up some serious injuries – it took me a good three months to recover.

I only found out all these details once I regained consciousness. At the time I didn't know anything – either about how bad my injuries were, or the accident being reported in the papers. A full week after I'd been rushed to hospital, I was still lying there flat out, unconscious, on the hospital bed. When I finally opened my eyes, the first thing I saw was my father, peering into my face. He was calling my name, over and over again: 'Mayumi! Mayumi!'

'Hey, Dad,' I said, apparently. 'I'm going to get married.' I've been told I had a radiant smile on my face. And then I conked straight out again.

Nobody believed my story: not my dad, nor the doctor, nor any of the nurses. 'The shock of the accident has rendered you unable to distinguish dream from reality,' they kept telling me, until finally even I began to wonder what the truth was. When I regained consciousness, that bit of transparent plastic that had been wrapped round my finger and that I'd been told would do for my wedding ring was no longer there. But I was determined to check things out for myself. As soon as I was discharged I decided I simply had to visit the site of the accident. The spot where I'd been run over was in a shopping arcade not two kilometres from my family home. That day when I ran away,

I'd been under the impression I was going off on a great big journey, but all I had really done was wander around from place to place in the streets where I lived.

The shopping arcade was 500 metres long, and I walked all 500 metres, hobbling on my crutches.

About ten metres from the entrance was a butcher's shop. There were some fresh deep-fried croquettes on sale at the front of the store, so I bought one and ate it on the spot, to check the taste. The instant I bit into it, I knew. There was no mistaking it. True, this croquette was piping hot and crisp, but it tasted exactly the same as the ones I had hooked out of the black plastic bag that night.

To the right of the butcher's shop was a vegetable and fruit shop. To the left was a pharmacy. In the space between the butcher's and the pharmacy, I could see a little alley, just wide enough for one person to go along. I went all the way up it, doing my best to avoid the rubbish and other odds and ends, and emerged onto a road with a notice that said Pedestrians and Bicycles Only. On the other side of the road, I could see a residential area with rows of identical houses.

Rows and rows of identically coloured roofs, identically shaped windows and identically painted walls. As far as the eye could see. Every house was fronted by a strong iron gate. I went to every one of those houses, and rang on the doorbells, and I asked as politely as I could using the intercom if this was the house where Jack lived.

But at every house I got the same answer.

'It most certainly is not!'

'No such person!'

'You've got the wrong house!'

If it happened to be a woman that replied, and she had a low voice, I wouldn't be able to contain myself, and I would just have to ask something else:

'Is that you, Mum?'

'And who might you be?' the other person would say.

'I'm Happy-chan!' I would reply.

'Clear off, or I'll call the police.'

This happened any number of times. Sadly, that's as far as I ever got. So I wasn't able to keep my promise, and I never saw Jack, ever again.

Ten years have now passed. These days, amazingly enough considering what an idler I used to be, I go out every day to work. I have to, in order to support my family. Every morning after I wave goodbye to my husband and child at the door, I pedal my bike to the factory where I have a part-time job. From 9 a.m. to 3 p.m., there I am, devotedly applying adhesive labels, one after another, onto bottles of hand cream. The job seems to fit my personality. If anyone were to ask me whether I find it fun and worthwhile, I would have no difficulty saying yes, I do! I love having to match the movements of my fingers and wrists to the repeated, predictable patterns of the equipment, I love getting my wages on the twentieth of every month, I love having to stand in a line every morning to exchange greetings with the other workers and then do radio callisthenics, I love eating my bento lunch gossiping with the other part-timers about our colleagues behind their backs. Really, who would have thought that going out and doing a day's work could be so much fun?

As for how my husband and I met, well, we were introduced as potential partners in a marriage interview seven years ago by a friend of my father's. Soon after we were married, my husband was relocated to a neighbouring prefecture, and so we moved to a different house. My father came along with us, but the following winter he suffered a stroke, and after two weeks spent unconscious in hospital he died. But not long after that, almost immediately in fact, our son came into the world. He has just this past month started primary school. My husband, who is three years older than me, is very enthusiastic about sports, and our son must have taken after him because there's nothing the boy loves more than being physically active, and so in addition to the swimming and gymnastics he took up at age three, just recently he's started to show an interest in playing football. The cost of the tutoring for all these sports mounts up, but my husband and I tend to think, well, if our son wants to give something a go, we'd like to do all we can to support him.

These days I'm rushed off my feet, what with my part-time job and all the many tasks I have to do as a housewife, and the days go by in a flash. It seems incredible, considering the way I once was, but these days the more rushed I am, the more fulfilled I feel my life to be. It makes you think, doesn't it – how a person's life really is so full of surprises. I am now a quite ordinary busy housewife leading a comfortable, peaceful life; I have a husband who is kind and considerate, and an adorable little son . . . There is not a single thing I regret, or feel wistful about. Not a single thing.

Still, just occasionally, certain thoughts do flicker through my mind . . . Just sometimes, as I put together the food for my lunch box, or hang washing out to dry on my balcony, or sit astride my bicycle waiting for the traffic lights to turn green, or when I'm in the midst of ironing my husband's shirts . . . I will start to think.

I wonder how he is doing these days?

I wonder if he's smiling? I wonder if he's angry with me? Maybe he's crying. Perhaps, having given in to Noboru's insistence, he has found another special someone . . . I wonder if that special someone has had babies – if she has given birth to a King, a Toad, or a Gorimaru?

Or could it be that he is still there waiting for me, pining for me, in that room . . . hoping that I will fulfil the promise that I made . . .

The way his whiskers felt when we touched that night is still there, a clear sensation on the tip of my nose.

AFTERWORD
BY
SAYAKA MURATA

Translated by Ginny Tapley Takemori

I'm walking outside. There is a big, wide 'blue sky', and a pleasant 'breeze'. There is an expanse of 'lawn' in the 'park'. I use my 'mouth' to breathe, and move my 'legs' to walk, and I am drinking 'water' from a flask in my 'hand'. Ever since I was born, I have been surrounded by things with names, not feeling any sense of incongruity in my 'daily life'.

But beneath the world that has been converted into language, another realm in which there are no names exists: a realm of emotions, sights, bodies, sensations, substances and awareness. We may appear to be missing out on this realm, but our subconscious is keenly aware of it, and it continues to be there right behind the verbalised reality without ever being negated or discovered. When I first read 'Asa: The Girl Who Turned Into a Pair of Chopsticks' in a magazine, I felt shock and also relief. The story made me aware of an intimate and beloved unknown that had always been with me. It was a familiar, pressing sensation that I couldn't just ascribe to having read a 'strange story' and leave it at that. An unnamed memory ached and began to blossom in my body, and everything I'd always thought I had been 'seeing' was now being turned inside out as the world perceived by my unconscious began to raise its voice. This is what the story meant to me, and why I found it so uniquely special.

Natsuko Imamura is an author I particularly cherish. There are many aspects of our existence, and of myself, that only the words in her stories can allude to, and reading them I remember how very important I somehow feel these things to be. To see her words touch upon these obscure aspects envelops me in a sensation that feels as though surprise and relief have fused into a quiet vibration. The words 'strange' and 'mysterious' are not enough to describe the joy this gives me as a reader.

There are three stories in this book. Just reading a summary of them will probably give readers the impression that they are strange stories happening in a distant place. But I feel each of these stories is keenly connected to myself, and I am struck with an odd sense of nostalgia. The stories have been spun in words from the Japanese language; the words line up into paragraphs, impressed on paper in a liquid called ink; the pages stack up and are bound into books that in turn are displayed in bookshops; and one of those books has been picked up by this reader and taken home. That in itself feels like an allegory, as though they are very important stories that I've been seeking for a long time. The reason I feel this way is that Imamura's stories are imbued with a magical power that takes the reader out of their comfort zone and connects them with the uncharted world that they were actually familiar with all along.

This custom of having another author write about a work for an afterword placed awkwardly at the end of the book has always felt somewhat crass to me. If anyone happens to turn to these pages first, I want them to close the book, take a deep breath, then open it up at the beginning and fully savour with their entire body the stories in this collection. Certain wonderful stories have the power to become the reader's 'own story'. I feel that Imamura's work has this particular kind of charm. Upon finishing the stories, the reader might not want to read what someone else has to say about them, in which case there is no need to read what I've written here. Please just close the book and savour Imamura's words alone. Of course, readers should be free to read a novel in whatever way they like. Then what am I doing here writing this afterword? It's only because Imamura's works are always quiet miracles for me personally. That makes me not want to interfere with other readers' miracles. This book has the power to make me hope I won't.

When I first read the title story of this collection, Asa's passion and excitement once she has become chopsticks struck me like words I had been seeking for a long time. I put the magazine on my bookcase in a place where my eye would most naturally be drawn to it so that I could open up its pages and re-encounter the story at any time. I wanted to be always connected to it, and would feel anxious if I couldn't see it on the shelf. It made me feel like I wanted to live inside the world of the story. The fact I felt this way meant that before reading the story, I was living in a world in which the story didn't exist. Both worlds were lonely, but the loneliness without this story and loneliness generally felt like utterly different worlds to me.

What all of these three stories share is that the border between reality and illusion is blurred without any sense of incongruity, and the stories seem all the more true to life for this. I even ended up wondering why I'd ever thought there was a border between the real world and the daydream world to begin with. The world we call 'real' includes delusion and illusion, strange words and a lot of things that are unexplainable, and in the 'illusory' world there are numerous things like a startling vividness, smells, sensations, sounds, tastes and music that are even more real than in 'reality'. Why had I ever drawn a line between them? Before I knew it I had lost a sensibility that until then I'd taken for granted, and with this loss another world had become visible. Loss is a type of gain, I thought as I gazed at the new sights that lay beyond the book.

These stories give the reader another way of seeing. While living as a human, without realising it, your brain, and information, and knowledge, and memory, all insert themselves into the way you see things, transfiguring what you should be seeing, and sometimes contaminating it. Sights contaminated by the brain and knowledge give people the sensation they correctly understand the world, which is reassuring. In fact, though, an uncontaminated gaze exists in everyone. That 'eye' quietly continues to capture the world as it is before being transfigured by knowledge.

The three stories make the reader hyperaware of what is continually being captured by their gaze separate from the brain, humanity, information. This is why the view they provide always feels familiar, even if unknown and mysterious. They bring a kind of universality that is not merely strange. And this is why I think that Imamura's stories will come as extraordinary miracles for many people.

I would also like to mention the power of the words from which these stories have been spun. Even though they are words that I also use all the time and am used to, in the stories they have an absolutely different appearance and presence in the surprising way they are placed. These words are sucked up through my eyes and come falling into my body, often startling me. It's not only the world or the gaze that have different angles but also words, and I shiver in raptures at how, seen from other angles, the words linger in this book sometimes bewitchingly, and at other times bizarrely. It is as though the miracle of reading has itself become a living creature within this book, and this is its charm.

Now this book is coming out in a new format, and again I give thanks for this new miracle. I am truly happy to be in a world in which *Asa: The Girl Who Turned Into a Pair of Chopsticks* now exists.

CREDITS

'Asa: The Girl Who Turned Into a Pair of Chopsticks': 'Ki ni natta Asa', originally published in the literary journal *Bungakukai* in October 2017.

'Nami, Who Wanted to Get Hit (and Eventually Succeeded)': 'Mato ni natta Nami', originally published in the journal *Bungakukai* in November 2020.

'A Night to Remember': 'Aru yo no omoide', originally published in *Bungaku Mook: Taberu no ga Osoi*, Volume 5, April 2018.